"What do we do now, Tyler?"

Kara whispered.

"I suppose we could claim we were quarreling, like we'd planned."

"Even I wouldn't believe that one, and this story is my invention."

"Well, what then?"

Kara pulled a face. "I don't know. Maybe we can..."

Just then, Tyler saw everyone else rush out of the house. Mark was pointing at them.

"Go to plan B." Tyler finished her sentence with a self-deprecating smirk, grabbed Kara and pulled her into a full embrace. As he bent to kiss her, he whispered a warning against her lips. "Hang on. This won't hurt a bit."

Books by Valerie Hansen

Love Inspired

The Wedding Arbor #84
The Troublesome Angel #103
The Perfect Couple #119

VALERIE HANSEN

was thirty when she awoke to the presence of the Lord in her life and turned to Jesus. In the years that followed she worked with young children, both in church and secular environments. She also raised a family of her own and played foster mother to a wide assortment of furred and feathered critters.

Married to her high school sweetheart since age seventeen, she now lives in an old farmhouse she and her husband renovated with their own hands. She loves to hike the wooded hills behind the house and reflect on the marvelous turn her life has taken. Not only is she privileged to reside among the loving, accepting folks in the breathtakingly beautiful Ozark Mountains of Arkansas, she also gets to share her personal faith by telling the stories of her heart for Steeple Hill's Love Inspired line.

Life doesn't get much better than that!

The Perfect Couple
Valerie Hansen

Published by Steeple Hill Books™

STEEPLE HILL BOOKS

Steeple
Hill™

ISBN 0-373-87125-2

THE PERFECT COUPLE

Copyright © 2000 by Valerie Whisenand

Visit us at www.steeplehill.com

Printed in U.S.A.

Blessed are they that mourn,
for they shall be comforted.
—*Matthew 5:4*

To Joe, for being a great husband and father and also being substitute "daddy" to Whiskers, Harry (also known as Poopsie), Splash, Blackie, Neek, Gypsy, Dumbo, Essence, Dinky, Duchess, Beans, Shady, Big Molly and Little Molly.
Thankfully, not all at the same time!

Chapter One

~

Kara Shepherd loosed her ponytail and slipped the clip into the pocket of her jeans. Weary, she rubbed the back of her neck. It had been a long day. And it wasn't over. Sighing, she picked up the inventory list and went to work.

Intent on counting the supplies in exam room three, she didn't hear anyone approach. The first hint that she wasn't alone was a light tap on her shoulder.

She shrieked, whirled, her heart thudding. It took only an instant to realize who had innocently tapped her. "Oh, my!" Air whooshed out of her lungs all at once, leaving her breathless. "Susan, you startled me."

"Boy, no kidding. I thought for a minute there you were going to slug me!"

"Not a chance." Kara was still working to catch

her breath. She managed a smile. "I'd never do anything like that to my favorite sister."

"I'm your *only* sister."

"Good point." Her grin grew. Mischief lit her brown eyes; the same lovely eyes her sibling had. "But don't push your luck by sneaking up on me like that again. I wanted a brother, you know."

"And I wanted a puppy. Maybe I should have been the veterinarian in the family instead of you."

Kara reached out and gave her sister a hug. "I'm glad we're related. You're very special to me. I don't know what I'd have done without you, after—"

"Hey, no sweat. I like working here." Susan hugged her tight, then stepped away. "Which reminds me. I finished all the billing. I figured I'd stop by the post office on my way home and mail everything. Want to come to dinner tonight?"

Kara wasn't fooled by her sister's overly casual manner. She knew Susan had purposely changed the subject for her benefit, to get her mind off her supposed loss. *If only she knew. If only someone did.*

Kara felt like a fraud every time she accepted an expression of sympathy. In truth, she was a lot less sorrowful than she should be about losing Alex, and her secret awareness of that fact left her feeling decidedly uncomfortable, especially at times like these.

"Well?"

Susan's voice drew Kara back to the present. "Um, no, thanks. I still have a lot to do here."

"Like what? Count pills? Roll bandages? Mop the floor?"

Kara chuckled. "Mop? When I have a hired slave like you to do it for me?"

"Yeah, yeah. Rub it in. You always were a pain."

"Isn't that what little sisters are for?"

"Maybe. If I ever manage to get pregnant and have a girl, I'll know if the problem was all little girls or just *you*."

"If your baby's half as nice as you and Mark are, she'll be perfect. Now go on home and leave me in peace." Kara put her hands on Susan's shoulders, turned her and urged her out the exam room door.

Susan led the way down the hall. "You really aren't coming to dinner?"

"Nope. If I keep you from having any time alone with that handsome husband of yours I'll never be an aunt. Besides, I've had dinner with you three times this week already."

"You're avoiding the ranch, aren't you? You just don't want to run into Tyler Corbett."

They had reached the deserted waiting room. Kara unlocked the heavy glass front door and held it open for her sister. "He doesn't scare me."

"Oh, no. You just hate each other's guts, that's all."

Kara frowned. "I don't hate anybody." She paused, sighed. "Not anymore."

Waving the bundle of outgoing bills, Susan said, "I'm sending him another notice."

"I told you not to do that. Mark's job as his foreman is more important than collecting on a bad debt."

Susan shook her head. "Look, Kara, if Corbett fires Mark because of a bill from you...which he owes, by the way...then he's a bigger fool than I thought. Trust me. I've gotten to know the man since we moved into the house on the ranch. I'm sure he's not vindictive."

"Humph. I wish I could agree with you. The last time I saw him he avoided me like I was his worst enemy."

"Hey, that sounds like an answer to a prayer to me," Susan said. "You didn't want to get stuck making polite conversation with him, did you?"

As always, her sister was the voice of reason. Kara patted her on the shoulder. "No, I guess not. Thanks for reminding me who's in charge of my life. I tend to get caught up in other things and forget."

"You'll be back on track soon, now that you've started going to church again," Susan assured her. "You'll see."

"I suppose so." She brushed a goodbye kiss on her cheek. "Now get going. I don't want Mark thinking I work you too hard."

"Right. I'll stop by your place and feed your animals for you. See you in the morning." As she climbed into her car she called back, "And don't forget to eat dinner!"

"I have a brownie in my desk drawer if I get desperate," Kara shouted, waving. "I'll be fine."

Watching her sister drive away, Kara locked the door and leaned against it for a few moments, thinking. Remembering. It *had* felt right to be back in the church in Hardy again after nearly two years' absence. The congregation had been wonderful. They'd welcomed her with open arms, accepting her as if she'd never been gone.

Kara made a derisive sound. Well, *most* of them had. The lone dissenter had been Tyler Corbett. They'd both been on their way out of the sanctuary one recent Sunday morning and their glances had met by accident. The brief, intense look he'd given her before turning away could have wilted the beautiful flower arrangement in front of the altar!

Working was Kara's favorite diversion. She often stayed long after the veterinary hospital closed, using her job as an excuse to escape the memories that still lingered in her house. The house she and Alex had shared. As his widow she didn't need all the room the old farm in Peace Valley provided but the place was paid for, so she'd stayed. Truth to tell, until she got her practice back on a more solid financial footing, she couldn't afford to move.

She had briefly considered hiring another large-animal vet to replace Alex, while she continued seeing the dogs, cats and assorted other smaller critters, as before. Then her flighty receptionist had quit and she'd had all she could handle to keep up with the office work, until Susan had arrived in Arkansas and volunteered to step into the job. After that, it had seemed to Kara that the practice was just as it should be and she'd abandoned the idea of adding anyone else to the staff.

She sighed. Looking back, it was easy to see that the Lord had been with her, even in the worst days of her marriage. And He was still looking after her.

"Thank you for everything, Father. Especially for sending Susan," she whispered.

Looking up at the darkening sky through the window opposite her desk, Kara noted gray clouds across the horizon. Evening storms were common in that part of the Ozarks, especially in the spring, but they could be frightening to some of her overnight patients. The dogs and cats were already anxious because they were separated from their owners. Thunder and lightning only made things worse.

"And thank you, Lord, that I'm still here tonight," she added, heading for the kennel area. A few kind words or even a mild tranquilizer would make the poor animals' night much easier.

She was petting a mongrel with a broken leg when she heard an echoing thud. Assuming it was the beginnings of thunder, she ignored the noise. Then it came again. Louder this time and accompanied by shouting. Male shouting.

Pausing, she listened. The dogs in the kennel runs had begun to bark but she could still make out a few words. Whoever the man was, he had a pretty colorful vocabulary.

Following the sound of the pounding, Kara stopped at the rear door. It was solid wood, not like the glassed-in front of the animal hospital, so she couldn't see who was making all the racket. Unwilling to unlock the door since she was there alone, she called out, "Who is it?"

"Open up," the man demanded. "It's an emergency."

"Go around to the front," Kara instructed. At least that way she could see who she was dealing with and make a sensible decision about whether or not it would be safe to let him in.

He mumbled something unintelligible, then said, "I was already there once."

"Well, go there again."

"I should have known I'd get this kind of treatment from you," he shouted through the heavy door. "Have a heart. It's raining."

Kara listened. The staccato sound of drops hitting the metal roof confirmed the man's statement. Since the porch where he now stood was dry, he did have a valid excuse for not wanting to circle the building. When she was in the kennel area she seldom heard anything over the uproar of barking and mewing, so it was highly likely he actually had knocked on the front door, just as he'd claimed. Which meant he was probably harmless.

Still cautious, Kara unlocked the door and opened

it wide enough to peek out. Her eyes widened. Tyler Corbett? It couldn't be!

She blinked as she combed a fall of hair back off her forehead with her free hand. It certainly was him. And he looked anything but cordial. His jacket was wet, water was dripping off the brim of his cowboy hat, and his scowl was even more pronounced than it had been the last time they'd met.

"What do you want?" she asked firmly.

"A pepperoni pizza." His tone was sarcastic. "With extra cheese."

Kara tried to slam the door. The toe of Tyler's boot stopped it from closing. "I don't like jokes," she told him. "Now go away."

"Not till you help this poor dog."

"What poor dog?" She let the door swing open and stuck her head out far enough to scan the whole porch. "I don't see any dog."

"He's in here." Tyler looked down.

Kara's gaze followed his. His arm was bent to support a slight bulge on one side of his jacket. When he lifted the fabric away from his chest, Kara could see the dark, soulful eyes of a floppy-eared, nondescript brown puppy.

"Why didn't you say so?" She quickly threw the door wide-open and ushered him inside. "Follow me. I'll have a look."

Tyler kicked the door closed behind him, took off his soggy hat and reluctantly trailed her down the hall. He hadn't intended to do more than drop off the pup and go home. If he hadn't thought the dog's condition was critical, he wouldn't have brought it to that particular animal hospital in the first place. And he certainly wouldn't be taking any orders from Kara Shepherd.

She moved lightly, with athletic grace, he noted, watching her precede him. Funny. He'd seen her before but he'd never noticed that. Nor had he seen how long and silky her hair was when it was unbound. He'd also never noticed what a take-charge person she could be. About the only times he'd talked to her was when she'd acted as her husband's assistant during veterinary visits to the cattle at his ranch in Ash Flat. She'd seemed more introverted then.

Kara led him to the closest exam room and gestured toward a stainless steel table. "Put him there."

"He's awful cold," Tyler said. He dropped his hat on a chair. "And I'm not sure how busted up he might be. I think it's pretty bad."

His concern brought her up short. So, there was a tender bone in Mr. Corbett's body after all. Well, well. What a surprise.

She reached into a cabinet beneath the supply rack and brought out a fluffy white towel, draping it over the exam table. "Okay. Lay him on this to begin with. If I need to do anything serious, we'll move him into surgery."

Tyler began to slowly part the front of his coat

and lean toward the towel. The puppy whimpered. "I'm afraid to move him much."

"Here. I'll help." She circled the table without thought and reached for the jacket, folding it back carefully. There seemed to be more blood on the man's shirt and coat lining than there was on the dog.

Kara took a moment to caress the puppy's face and check his gums for color. Thankfully, they were pink and healthy. He hadn't lost too much blood.

"That's a good boy. I'm your friend, too," she cooed, sliding one hand along the length of his body and lifting gently. "Come on. That's it. You'll be just fine."

Tyler leaned toward her, bending over the exam table, and together they maneuvered the injured dog out of the crook of his arm.

Kara continued speaking softly to reassure the puppy as she eased him down onto the towel. "That's good. Almost there."

"Watch that front leg," Tyler warned. "I think it may be broken." He reached out to cradle the tiny bones. Kara did the same. Their hands accidentally touched.

She looked up, startled. Tyler was staring back at her as if he'd never seen her before. "You can let go, now," she finally managed to say. "I've got him."

"Right. I was just..." He frowned. "Never mind."

Well, at least he didn't look angry anymore, she thought, relieved. She quickly refocused on the job at hand. "He's in shock, like you thought. That's why he was acting so cold. You probably saved his life by keeping him warm the way you did."

"I didn't know what else to do. By the time I found him, he looked like he'd been there for some time. When I picked him up he started bleeding again."

Kara was swabbing the matted fur around the wounds with peroxide as she assessed her patient. "There's one deep laceration on his shoulder and a few other smaller ones. I suspect you were right about the broken leg. Can't tell yet about internal damage. How was he hurt?"

"I think a car hit him. I found him by the side of the road."

She nodded. "These injuries are consistent with that kind of an accident. How long have you had him?"

Tyler pushed up the sleeve of his jacket and looked at his watch. "About fifteen minutes, give or take."

"What?" She froze in midmotion.

"He's not my dog."

"I see. Do you know who he belongs to?"

"Not a clue. I suppose he was dumped. Lots of folks seem to think that the country is a wonderful place to abandon unwanted animals."

"I know what you mean. I got three of my own

dogs that way. No telling how many others just wandered off and starved to death.''

"Or became a coyote's dinner.''

"Don't remind me.'' She shivered. So did the pup.

"Will you be able to save him?''

"I think his chances are good. He's young. That's definitely in his favor. We'll start by sewing up the gash in his shoulder, then X-ray the leg to see if it needs a splint or a cast.''

Tyler raised one dark eyebrow. "We?''

"A figure of speech.''

"Oh.''

"However...'' She did need help. And he was handy. There was nothing wrong with having him assist her. Besides, he'd always been disgustingly overbearing. It might be fun to turn the tables for a change, to see how he behaved in a situation where he wasn't the one giving all the orders.

A slight smile lifted the corners of Kara's mouth. She bent over the puppy, letting her long, brown hair sweep across her cheeks to hide her amusement until she could get it under control. "I could give him a general anesthetic instead of a local, but I'm afraid his already depressed nervous system might shut down if I do. That's why I'd rather not operate to pin the leg bones.''

"Sounds logical. So?''

"So, I'll need you to hold him still while I work.''

"I have a lot to do at the ranch,'' he alibied.

"Fine." She straightened, managed to face him soberly. "I'll call Susan to come back in. Even if she's home, it could take her a while to get here, though. I'd rather do what's best for the dog."

"Which is?"

"Start immediately. You don't have to help. I can always chase him around the hospital with a needle and sutures while he hops along on a broken leg."

"Very funny."

"Just making a point." Kara's smile crept back. Mischief lighted her eyes. "Well?"

Muttering under his breath, Tyler shed his coat and began to roll up his sleeves. "Okay. You win. What do I do first?"

Kara was amazed at how competent her drafted assistant turned out to be. All she had to do was tell him once and he did whatever she said. Correctly. His compassion for the injured little dog was even more impressive.

They had successfully tended to the puppy's wounds, X-rayed his leg and started to set it. As soon as the bones were stabilized the pup had settled right down, exhausted.

Up to her wrists in the slippery solution that was part of the new, lightweight casting material, Kara realized she'd forgotten to pull back her hair and it was getting in the way. She blew it out of her eyes, tossed her head, rubbed her cheek against one shoulder.... Nothing worked.

Tyler was steadying the sleepy puppy, gently stroking its head and leaning close to speak softly to it as if Kara weren't there. "Your doctor's got a problem, kid. Yes, she does. I think she needs a haircut."

She tried her best to ignore the taunt. A wild hair stuck to the perspiration on her forehead and tickled her lashes. When she tried to wipe it away with her forearm, it whipped into her right eye. Squeezing that eye tightly shut, she wished mightily for a second pair of hands. Hands that didn't belong to smart aleck Tyler Corbett.

"I think she's winking at me," he told the pup. "Either that or she's making eyes at you." He glanced up at Kara, giving her a lopsided grin. "Want some help?"

That was the last straw. "Oh, no. I'll just sit here and go blind while my hands become a permanent part of this dog's cast."

"I take it that was a yes."

"Yes." She made a contrite face. "Please."

"That's better. I hate it when people aren't specific. What do you want me to do? Cut it off?"

"My hair? No!" she snapped back without thinking. His resultant chuckle aggravated her. Of course he hadn't intended to actually cut her hair! How dense could she be?

Kara pulled herself together, helped by the fact that her eye was really beginning to smart. "There's a big clip in the right-hand pocket of my jeans. Use that.''

Hesitating, Tyler raised one dark eyebrow and eyed the slim hips encased in form-fitting denim. "I don't suppose you could hand it to me, could you?"

"Of course not." Kara suddenly understood exactly what was stopping him and her cheeks warmed in a bright blush. "Tell you what. Why don't you just come over here and hold the hair back for a few minutes. Get it out of my eyes. I'm almost done."

Tyler wasn't in any hurry to accommodate her. He was still recovering from the bewilderment he'd felt when their hands had touched. Just because he was a widower and Kara Shepherd was a widow didn't mean he was interested in forming any kind of relationship with her. Or with any woman, for that matter. There would never be anyone like his Deanne. She'd been the perfect wife. Practically a saint.

Which meant he'd certainly be immune to any mild charm a prickly person like Kara might have, he reasoned logically. Pulling her hair back for her would be no more exciting than combing the tail of his favorite Quarter horse.

Reassured, he sauntered around the table. "Okay. No sweat."

"Thanks." She leaned her head to one side. "It's this eye that hurts. See if you can clear that first, will you?"

Tyler lifted his hand. Hesitated. Discovered he actually wanted to see what it felt like to touch that beautiful, silky hair. Until now, that kind of act had been reserved for his late wife. Transferring those feelings to any other woman was totally unacceptable.

Kara peered over her shoulder as best she could without letting go of the puppy's cast. "Well? This stuff is hardening. What are you waiting for?"

What, indeed? He didn't even like this woman. Surely, there was no reason to avoid touching her. He leaned closer so he could see the fine hairs against her cheek, reached out and carefully swept them back.

A tingle danced across Kara's face and skittered down her spine. His fingertips were rough, yet his touch was light, barely there. It was amazing that a man that big, that imposing, could be so gentle when he wanted to be. She shivered, aware of his closeness, of his breath on her cheek as he examined her eye.

"Did I get the hair out?" he asked quietly.

"I—I think so. Thanks."

Tyler straightened. Stepping behind her he carefully gathered the rest of her hair in both hands and held it back while she worked. "Okay. Just hurry up, will you? I've got other things to do besides hang around here." He knew his words sounded unduly harsh, especially since Kara was being a Good Samaritan, but he didn't like the feelings she'd awakened in him and he wanted to escape from her influence as soon as possible.

She continued to smooth the cast, glad the job was nearly done, because she could barely think straight with him standing so close. He made her miss the quiet companionship of a husband. Even one like Alex.

She blinked and sniffled, blaming the moisture pooling in her eyes on irritation from the stray hair.

Still holding her hair, Tyler leaned closer. "You all right?"

Kara felt his breath tickle her ear. She searched for words, *any* words, to answer and found none. His presence filled the room, overwhelmed her. All she'd have to do was turn her head and...

And what? Make a fool of herself? She was just overtired and stressed out. She must be. Only temporary insanity would make her think of Tyler Corbett as romantic.

She sniffled again, stalling for time to get her errant emotions under better control. *Please, Lord,* she prayed silently, simply, *help me.*

No bolt from the sky came to rescue her. No mountains crumbled. No seas parted. Tyler still bent over her, and her heart continued to hammer. The only change in the room was the sudden wafting odor of...*pizza?*

Kara's head jerked toward the door. Tyler hadn't been ready for such an abrupt move and inadvertently pulled her hair. She yowled.

He let go and jumped back. "What the—?" His gaze followed Kara's.

Standing in the doorway, with a broad grin on her face and a pizza box in her hands, was her sister, Susan.

Chapter Two

Susan giggled. "Well, well. What have we here?"

"Not what it looks like," Kara countered. "Mr. Corbett found an injured dog and we were...I was...just setting its broken leg."

"Okay. If you say so." Susan laid the pizza box on a chair and stepped up to the table so she could steady the puppy. It licked her hand and she smiled down at it.

"I *do* say so," Kara insisted, stripping off her latex gloves and dropping them in the trash. "If I'd known you were coming back tonight, I'd have waited till you were here to help."

"Looks like you did okay without me." Her eyebrows arched as she glanced over Kara's shoulder at the flustered man who was doing his best to appear unconcerned. He'd thrust his hands into the pockets of his jeans, hiding them as if they might be considered evidence against him.

Now that the atmosphere in the small room was no longer romantic, Kara was easily able to resume her professional bearing. "Give that a few more minutes to set," she told Susan, gesturing at the puppy, "then put him in one of the empty cages up here. I want him close so I can observe him tonight, just in case he has internal injuries, too."

Tyler spoke up. "You're going to stay here? All night?"

"She does that all the time," Susan explained. "That's why I brought the pizza. I figured she'd need something to eat besides the one brownie left over from lunch."

"I didn't mean for you to have to go to so much extra trouble," Tyler said, addressing Kara. "I just didn't know what else to do with him. Once I spotted him, I couldn't drive off and let him die. I wouldn't have brought him here if there'd been any other vet hospital close by."

"Of course you wouldn't," she said, trying to ignore the implication.

"I didn't mean it like that."

"Don't apologize," she said flatly. "And don't worry about me. I have a couch in my office where I sleep whenever I have to stay over. I'll be fine." She turned her attention to the drowsy pup. "He looks good so far. I'll check on him every hour or so till I'm sure he's going to be all right."

Susan was glancing around the room. "Where's the paperwork?"

"Well..." Kara's expression was apologetic. "Would you believe we didn't get around to making any?"

"In a heartbeat," Susan said. She looked to Tyler. "I'll need a name to put on the cage for identification. What do you call him?"

He drew the fingers of one hand down his cheeks to his chin, thinking. "All I've called him so far is 'Road Kill.'"

"Okay," she said. "Road Kill Corbett, it is."

Kara interrupted. "You can't give that poor little innocent thing a name like that."

"Why not?" Tyler was grinning broadly, obviously pleased with his witty selection.

The boastful look on his face did something strange to Kara's usually even disposition, making her decide to say exactly what she was thinking. "Because it isn't fair. What's he ever done to deserve a terrible slur like that?"

"You mean besides get hit by a car and nearly die?" Tyler's brows knit above deep-brown eyes that punctuated the question.

"Oh, that," she said sweetly, smugly. "I didn't mean the Road Kill part. I meant Corbett."

"I thought he was never going to close his mouth," Susan said, smiling at her sister as they got the puppy settled in his cage and went back to straighten up the exam room together. "Did you see the look on the poor man's face?"

"See it? I'll never forget it. It was all I could do to keep from busting up laughing. If he hadn't stormed out of here when he did, I might have exploded!"

"I couldn't believe you had the nerve to say something like that in the first place. What came over you?"

"I don't know. I guess he made me mad when he told us he only came here because he had no other choice. I wasn't very Christian, was I?"

"No. But the whole situation sure was funny."

"It was, wasn't it?" She grew thoughtful. "When, exactly, did you decide I needed a pizza?"

"On my way home. Why?"

"Oh, no reason."

"Come on, Kara. We've been sisters for too long. You can't hide stuff from me and you know it. Fess up. Why is the pizza important?"

She busied herself wiping down the stainless steel table as she answered, "I just thought it might have been the answer to a prayer. But the timing's wrong. I didn't even ask for anything until long after you decided to come back."

"It could still be an answer."

"I don't see how."

Susan put her arm around her sister's shoulders. "Because God knows what we need before we even ask Him." She stopped being serious and added,

"Although, I must say, I've never asked Him to get me a pizza before."

"That wasn't what I prayed for."

"I figured as much. What was it you wanted? Me?"

"Sort of. I wasn't that specific."

"Then what?"

"You're not going to drop this subject till I tell you, are you?"

"Nope."

Kara made a face at her. "Okay. I'd prayed for a little help. That's all."

"With the puppy?" Puzzled, Susan studied her.

"Something like that." A blush warmed Kara's cheeks. She turned away, hoping Susan hadn't noticed, but she had.

"What? Tell me. Maybe I *can* help?"

Kara was sorely tempted to make up a problem rather than have to let Susan in on the truth. Instead, she opted for honesty. "I just wasn't comfortable with the situation, that's all."

"Because of Tyler Corbett? You weren't afraid of him, were you? Oh, don't be. Mark says he was so goofy in love with his late wife that he won't even *look* at another woman. The man's branded for life."

Kara understood completely. All her emotions blended together when she remembered Alex.

I won't ever let myself be hurt like that again, she vowed. Not ever again.

* * *

Susan had gone, leaving Kara to her thoughts and sole ownership of the now lukewarm pizza. Taking a piece of it with her, she strolled out to the waiting room to look over her practice and assess it while she ate.

Alex's death had left her with a lot of unpaid bills she hadn't expected. Most of those accounts had been settled but there was still the day-to-day running of the hospital to consider. Overhead like that wasn't cheap.

Susan had taken one look at the books and offered to work for no wages. Kara had insisted she be paid. As soon as they could afford to add another warm body, they planned to get a kennel boy—or girl—to keep the runs and cages clean. Until then, they shared the dirty work, too.

Sighing, she switched off the office light. Darkness had frightened Kara before she'd married Alex. After a few months with him, however, she'd welcomed the dark as a place to hide whenever he got so angry he lost control and began screaming at her. Living with him had been like sharing her life with a time bomb.

She was about to return to check on her latest patient when she saw headlights and the shadow of a truck bearing down on the glassed-in front of the animal hospital.

Startled, she stepped back just in case the driver misjudged the distance and didn't stop in time. Whoever it was, he sure was in a hurry. She wasn't up to tackling another emergency. Yet she knew she wouldn't—couldn't—turn anyone away.

The truck slid to a halt in a shower of mud reflected in the outside light. Someone jumped out and ran up the steps to the porch.

Kara dropped the slice of pizza into the trash, reached for her keys, and headed for the door. When she looked up she was face-to-face with Tyler Corbett. He was waving a white slip of paper.

She unlocked the door.

He burst through, his boots thudding on the tile floor. "I thought you didn't answer the door at night."

"I do when I can see who it is. What's wrong?" She followed him down the hall.

When he got to the place where light from her office illuminated the paper in his hand he stopped and whirled to face her. "This," he said, waving the paper.

Kara stood her ground. "Well, if you'll hold it still, I'll take a look."

"You don't have to look, *Doctor*," he said, exaggerating her title. "You sent it to me."

"I what?" Suddenly, she realized what he had to be holding. Except he couldn't be. Not yet. Susan had only put the monthly statements in the mail that evening.

"Whoa," Kara said firmly. "That's impossible."

"Oh? Then what's this?"

"Well, it looks like one of our bills but it can't be. The postal service isn't that good."

"This didn't come in the mail," Tyler said. "It was hand delivered." He unfolded the bill and held it up in front of her face. "Look at the part on the bottom. If you wanted me to pay for the puppy's care up front, you should have said so when I was here, not fired off a new bill before I even had a chance to drive all the way home!"

Susan. Kara's shoulders sagged. Of course. Her sister knew how badly she needed to keep her accounts current and in a fit of efficiency, she'd changed Tyler Corbett's bill to reflect the latest charges and hand delivered it to him, rather than put it in the mail with the others.

"I'm really sorry," Kara said. "She...we... shouldn't have done that."

"Well, you're right about that." He reached into his pocket and pulled out a wad of crumpled money, thrusting it at her. "Here. Consider this a down payment. If there are more charges before the dog gets well, I'll pay whatever it costs. In spite of what you seem to think, I'm not a deadbeat."

"This isn't necessary." Cupping the bills in both hands so she wouldn't drop them, she realized she was trembling. "You can write me a check later. When everything's done."

"No way, lady. I came here to pay up and I intend to do just that. Your brother-in-law works for me, remember? The last thing I need is to have my foreman think I'm dishonest.''

"I'm sorry. I'll see that Susan doesn't do anything like this again," Kara promised, chagrined. Her voice grew more faint. "It wasn't fair."

That sincerely apologetic attitude gave Tyler pause. The woman wasn't acting nearly as mercenary as he'd imagined she would. She hadn't even pocketed the money he'd shoved at her.

He had an attack of conscience. "I'm sorry, too. I didn't mean to scare you."

"You didn't," she said.

"Then why are you shaking?"

Kara stood taller, her chin jutting out, and alibied, "I'm probably just hungry."

"Didn't you eat that pizza?"

"I managed half a slice before you got here."

"Well, no wonder you're shaky. Come on." Without waiting for her consent, he ushered her into her office where the open pizza box rested in plain sight atop a file cabinet. He took the money from her hands, tossed it onto her desk and said, "You go wash up. I'll wait here."

"That's not necessary," Kara insisted. "I'm fine."

"No, you're not. And it's my fault. First I made you work overtime, then I kept you from enjoying your dinner." He scanned the office. "Got a microwave?"

"In the back. I use it to warm food for some of the animals." The wary look on his face made her smile in spite of her unsteadiness. "It's perfectly clean if that's what you're worried about. Anyway, I prefer my pizza cold."

"Good. Me, too. Go wash up while I find us some napkins."

"Us?"

Tyler shot her a lopsided smile. "If you don't mind, I'll join you. I was so busy blowing my stack I forgot to eat. I've just realized I'm famished."

Kara shrugged. "Sure. Why not?" Taking a deep, settling breath she left the room. There was no way she could tell anyone, especially not Tyler Corbett, why she'd been trembling. Hunger had nothing to do with it. When he'd burst in and shouted at her, her panicked response had been instinctive. Fresh fear had taken control. Alex's legacy of intimidation lived on.

After two years, she'd thought she was through being frightened. Tonight, when Tyler had confronted her, uncalled-for dread had returned as if it had never left.

Procrastinating, she splashed water on her face at the bathroom sink and stared into the mirror. "I'm going to be okay," she said to the image. "I'm smart and capable and I can make it on my own. It doesn't matter what Alex thought. He can't hurt me anymore."

And God loves you, she heard echoing in her head, in her heart. Kara nodded as she reached for a towel to dry her face. Remembering that she was a child of God was the most important part of her ongoing healing. It was His opinion that was important. No one else's counted.

"I looked in on Road Kill while you were gone," Tyler said. "He's asleep. I watched and he's breathing fine."

"I know. I checked him just before you charged in."

Tyler shrugged. "Yeah, well, I'm sorry about that. I'd had a pretty rough day. I had to throw away my favorite shirt and I'll probably have to give up my good jacket, too, thanks to the mess he made of it when I was trying to keep him warm."

"You don't need to throw the clothes away. A little household hydrogen peroxide will get rid of those stains. I use it all the time." She walked over to the file cabinet and picked up the flat, white pizza box, then returned to him and held it out. "Here. Help yourself. I could never eat all this anyway."

"Are you positive? Now that I think about it, I feel kind of bad about inviting myself."

"Nonsense. Somebody has to clean up the leftovers. If it hadn't been you, it would have been someone else."

Tyler took one slice and laid it on a paper towel.

"You mean you have a steady stream of clients pounding on your door at all hours, begging for food?"

"Not as a rule. I was thinking of my dogs at home. They love leftovers." She placed the box on her desk and served herself.

"I'm taking food out of the mouths of your pets?"

"I won't tell if you don't. Besides, this has pepperoni on it. It doesn't agree with them."

"Oh, I get it." He started to smile. "Protect the dogs by feeding the spicy stuff to the testy client."

"Something like that." Circling the desk she plopped down in the leather chair and leaned back, pizza in hand. It was strange to be sharing an impromptu meal with a man again. The fact that they were alone in her office, the office that used to belong to Alex, made the encounter seem even more bizarre.

With that thought, Kara's appetite vanished. She laid the pizza aside on a paper towel and tried to suppress a shiver. Tyler Corbett wasn't acting at all intimidating. Yet she found herself nervous, as if an obscure threat lurked in the otherwise tranquil environment.

Thoughts of her late husband continued to intrude and refused to go away. Alex wouldn't have liked her eating at this desk. His desk. Alex wouldn't have approved of sharing a meal with a client, either, even if the person was also a friend. And he'd have been absolutely furious if she'd opened the door after hours and welcomed a man who'd once threatened a lawsuit. A man like the one casually perched on the edge of the desk across from her. Her mouth went dry in response to her mental rambling.

Tyler noticed Kara's psychological retreat. One minute she'd been fine. The next, she was looking at him as if he were an escaped criminal, ready to hold a knife at her throat. As far as he could tell he hadn't done anything to trigger that kind of reaction, except raise his voice when he'd arrived. Surely, that couldn't be what was bothering her now. She'd seemed normal enough, even friendly, once he'd apologized.

Tyler got to his feet and wiped his hands on a paper towel. "Well, I guess I should be going." He expected Kara to observe polite custom and disagree before finally giving in when he insisted on leaving.

Instead, she stood and headed for the office door. "That's probably a good idea."

Dumbfounded, he stared after her. "Who put the burr under your saddle?"

"No one." Starting down the hall she called back, "I'll unlock the front for you."

There was nothing more to say. Tyler grabbed his hat and coat and stomped out the glass door as soon as she'd jerked it open. He strode quickly to his truck. Kara Shepherd might be good with animals but she sure lacked the normal social graces where people were concerned. No wonder she'd stuck with that underhanded bum she'd married. They'd been perfect for each other.

Tyler jammed the truck in reverse and floored it. It didn't matter what that woman thought of him. After all, she was Shepherd's widow. The widow of the swindler who had cost him the health of his herd and nearly ruined everything he and Deanne had worked for.

He swung onto the highway. It would be just fine with him if he never had to deal with Dr. Kara Shepherd again, personally or professionally. And as soon as he got Road Kill bailed out, that was exactly how it was going to be.

Kara maintained her composure until Tyler was gone. Then she collapsed against the wall, hugging herself. What was it about her that brought out the worst in men? First her father. Then Alex. And now...

She wanted to weep, to wail, to wallow in self-pity. Blinking, she waited for the flood of tears that usually accompanied such poignant retrospection.

Nothing happened! No hysteria, no devastating gloom, not even one solitary tear.

Kara was astounded. She took a deep, slow breath. She was healing! The nightmare was finally coming to an end.

Overcome with a sense of God's presence she closed her eyes, lifted her hands in praise and accepted the gift with a whispered, "Oh, thank you, Father."

The simple prayer didn't begin to express the soul-deep joy suddenly filling her heart. Peace flowed over her, enveloping her in the warmth of her Heavenly Father's abiding, miraculous love.

Chapter Three

Kara wasn't in her office when Susan arrived the following morning. She tracked her down in the kennels and held out the handful of crumpled currency she'd found on the desk.

"What's all this?" Susan asked. "You moonlighting as a bank robber?"

"Nope. It's payment of a bill."

"Really? Hey, that's great!"

"No, it isn't." Kara scowled. "It came from Tyler Corbett."

Susan looked around quickly. "He's here?"

"Not any more. But he was last night. And he was *not* particularly impressed by your efficiency."

"Oops." She made a penitent face. "I get the idea you're not crazy about it, either."

"That's an understatement. Now he thinks I don't trust him to pay his debts."

"Well, you don't, do you?"

Kara took a moment to mull over the question. If she judged by their past association she shouldn't trust the man at all. Yet for some crazy reason, she did.

"I believe he'll pay for the puppy's care," she finally said. "As for what happened before, well, that was between him and Alex."

"But, I thought..."

"Nothing is certain where Alex was concerned," Kara said. "I know he did a lot of work for Corbett's ranch. But I don't know how accurate his record keeping was. That's why I dropped the idea to sue for the money after Alex died."

"You think he may have overcharged the ranch?"

Kara shrugged. "I hope not. Unfortunately, we'll never know for sure."

"But it is possible?" Susan was clearly disturbed by the thought.

"Oh, yes."

"I never dreamed Alex was like that."

Kara felt the urge to go on, to tell her sister everything. There was a great deal about Alex Shepherd that had remained hidden in the painful, private core of their supposedly perfect marriage. If she'd spoken out when Alex was living, maybe Susan could have offered some helpful advice. Now, however, the only benefit of confessing would be to know that someone else shared her suffering. Kara didn't want to lay that kind of burden on anyone.

She pressed her lips into a thin line. That wasn't completely true. She hadn't wanted advice or familial concern when Alex was alive. She still didn't. She'd purposely kept her misery to herself because she'd felt partly responsible for her bad marriage. Even now, that kind of thought kept nagging at the fringes of her consciousness, refusing to be banished.

Standing as tall as her five-foot-two-inch stature would allow, she said, "My husband is gone. I don't see any reason to discuss him, if you don't mind." The statement came out sounding so harsh she softened it with a tender smile and added, "Hey. Come on, Susan. It's a beautiful day and we should be praising the Lord that we have our whole lives ahead of us. Let's not dwell in the past, okay?"

To Kara's relief, her sister returned her smile and agreed. "Okay. It's a deal. So, let's talk about the patients. How's the infamous Road Kill Corbett doing this fine morning?"

"He's pretty chipper, considering. Last time I looked, he was happily shredding the newspapers we'd lined his cage with and tossing the soggy bits up in the air."

"Cute. Kind of like his owner, don't you think?"

Kara knew exactly what Susan was up to. Her loving but meddlesome older sister had been trying to play matchmaker for her ever since Susan had arrived in Arkansas. It was easier for Kara to pretend she'd misunderstood than it was to talk Susan out of continuing to do so.

"You'd know more about that than I do," Kara said sweetly. "You live on the Corbett ranch so you'd be far more likely to notice the condition of Mr. Corbett's newspapers after he's done reading them." She stifled a giggle.

"Very funny. You know I didn't mean Tyler tears up the paper with his teeth, like the puppy. What I meant was, don't you think he's kind of cute?"

"In what way?" Kara was determined to remain emotionally uninvolved. Anything to discourage her sister.

Susan threw up her hands. "I don't know. His eyes are gorgeous, so dark and brooding. And he has great hair. I wish Mark's was half as thick and nice."

"I can recommend a good coat conditioner," Kara teased. "It works wonderfully for all my dogs."

"You just aren't going to take me seriously, are you?"

"Why should I? You're not making any sense. First you tell me Mr. Corbett is still madly in love with his late wife, then you turn around and ask me if I find him attractive. That's ridiculous."

"Well—" Susan cast a sly smile her way "—nothing is carved in stone. Maybe he'll change his mind once he gets to know you better."

"No."

"Of course he will. You're smart, and pretty, and—"

Kara interrupted. "I mean, *no,* I don't intend to get to know the man any better than I already do. I've had enough of Tyler Corbett to last me a lifetime."

Susan was grinning. "I notice you didn't say you think he's ugly."

"He isn't ugly, he's—" Blushing, Kara broke off in midsentence.

"Aha! I thought so. You did notice how good-looking the guy is. Maybe there's hope for you yet."

"I am *not* interested in getting involved with another man, no matter how good he looks in a Stetson," Kara insisted. "Not ever. And certainly not a person as opinionated and short-tempered as Tyler Corbett."

"Don't be so sure. After all, just because a man isn't quiet and refined like Alex was doesn't mean he won't be every bit as easy to get along with, once you get to know him." Susan paused, studying her sister's pained expression. "What's the matter? What did I say? You look like you're about to cry."

Kara swallowed hard and steeled herself for the well-rehearsed denial she was ready to recite. Then it occurred to her that to do so would be to perpetuate a lie. What kind of practice of her faith would that be? Instead, she managed a smile and a diversion.

"I didn't get much sleep last night. I'm over-stressed." That was certainly true. She eyed the crumpled money Susan was still holding. "I had company, remember?"

"Did he yell at you?" Susan asked, chagrined.

"A little. Don't worry about it, okay?" Turning, Kara looped an arm around her sister's shoulders and guided her toward the front desk. "It's almost time to open and you haven't put out the display of flea collars that came in yesterday. Think you'll have time to do it this morning?"

"Sure. No sweat." Susan smiled slightly. "I'm sorry if I seemed too pushy. I just hate to see you all alone like this. I feel kind of sorry for Tyler, too, so I thought—"

"What part of *no* don't you understand?"

She brightened, her eyes twinkling. "Hey. I've got an idea. How about the new manager at the feed store? Would you like to meet him? I hear he's single."

"Susan…"

"Okay, okay. But you can't enjoy being a recluse. I know you too well to believe that. There's a man for you somewhere. I'll just have to keep looking till I find him."

"Aaargh!" Wheeling, Kara gave up and headed for the kennel. There was no reasoning with Susan when she was in one of her Ms.-Fix-It moods. As the younger of the two sisters, Kara had always looked up to Susan and admired her, even after they'd become adults. But this was one battle Susan was going to lose. No way was Kara going to allow herself to become romantically involved with another man. It was too scary an idea to even consider. She'd had her fill of men. And of marriage.

Shaking her head to punctuate her decision she made her way between the rows of smaller animal cages, her mind wandering. Yes, Tyler Corbett was good-looking. More than that, his tenderness toward helpless animals had spoken to her heart. But that was the end of her involvement. At this point, she didn't even care if she collected the full amount due for treatment of the injured pup he'd brought in. It would be worth it to write off the remainder of the bill if that meant she wouldn't have to face Tyler again.

Kara shivered. Truth to tell, she found she was actually starting to like him.

That inclination scared her far more than anything else had for a long, long time.

Kara was still insisting she wanted nothing to do with romance a week later, even though she was driving toward the Corbett ranch.

"This is all Susan's fault," she said to the drowsy puppy lying on the car seat beside her. "So help me, if she tries anything funny I'm going to disown her."

The pup thumped its thin tail and rested its chin on her lap, looking up at her with sad, brown eyes.

"If it wasn't for you," Kara told him, "I wouldn't be doing this." She laid her hand on his head and smoothed his fur. The cut by his ear was almost healed. His broken leg would take longer.

Recalling her recent conversation with her sister, Kara sighed in resignation.

"So, what are we going to do with Road Kill?" Susan had asked that morning. "We haven't had a single call on that lost-and-found ad you had me put in the paper."

Kara remembered making a face. "I don't know. I can't take him home with me. My neighbors are already complaining about the greyhound getting out and chasing game, and the rest of my dogs barking too much. Not to mention my cats hunting wild birds."

"Well," Susan had drawled, "I could always deliver him to Tyler." She paused and arched her eyebrows. "Of course, since Mark works for him it might be better if I didn't make him mad. Again."

"Meaning?" Kara had a feeling she wasn't going to like the answer.

"I just thought, if *you* took the pup out to the ranch, I'd be off the hook and Mark wouldn't have to defend my actions to his boss, like before." She began to pout. "I'm still in the doghouse over that bill I hand delivered."

"No doubt."

"Well?"

Kara's eyes narrowed as she studied her seemingly innocent sister. "No tricks."

"Cross my heart." Her index finger traced an invisible X on her chest. "I just want to find a good home for the poor puppy, that's all. There's plenty of room on the ranch and nobody cares how much noise those dogs make."

"Then you and Mark can take him," Kara said, certain she'd come up with the perfect solution.

"Sorry. Can't. It's not our house, remember? We're not supposed to have pets inside. And it would be too lonely for Road Kill, anyway."

"Then leave him outside."

"Where he can get into more trouble or get hurt, again? No way. Tyler has a big, fenced yard for his dog. It would be the perfect place for recuperation."

"You're not going to drop this, are you?"

Susan had stood her ground and grinned with self-satisfaction. "Nope. I'm right. Admit it."

Which was why Kara was now driving toward the Corbett ranch in spite of her misgivings. She stroked the puppy's head slowly, gently, taking care to avoid his sore ear. The contact was soothing to both of them. Before she knew it, she'd arrived.

She turned into the gravel drive and drove beneath the iron-work arch marking the main ranch entrance. The only other times she'd been there was when she and Alex had come to treat Tyler's cattle. It seemed strange to be visiting in a quasi-unofficial capacity.

The Corbett ranch had always been impressive. The main house was a sprawling, brick residence that rivaled any in the area for both style and size. This time, though, Kara noticed that the flower beds needed care and the perennial plants were wildly overgrown. Tyler apparently wasn't interested in gardening.

Parking directly in front of the house, she carefully lifted the puppy and started for the porch. "Lord, be with me," she prayed in a whisper. "And help me find the right words to soften his heart."

Before she could ring the bell, the door was jerked open.

Kara gasped. "Oh! You startled me."

"I wish I could say the same," Tyler countered. "Susan told me you were coming. I called your office as soon as I got back to the house to try to stop you. I'm afraid you've made the trip for nothing. I'm not taking that dog."

His pigheaded attitude provoked her. "Then why did you bother saving his life?"

"You know I couldn't just leave him there."

"But you have no qualms about leaving him homeless?"

"That's different."

"Not the way I see it." She stood her ground, her chin jutting out stubbornly, her eyes issuing a clear challenge.

"I hate to tell you this, but your opinion doesn't cut it with me, lady."

"Do you think I'm surprised?" she snapped back. "I don't care what you think of me, or my practice. All I care about right now is finding a place for this poor little helpless puppy to recuperate."

"So keep him at your place."

Kara arched her eyebrows. "I wish I could. Unfortunately, my neighbors are already upset about the menagerie I have out there."

"That's not my problem. It's yours."

"You're absolutely right." She extended her burden toward him and the pup began to wag its skinny tail excitedly. "And this one is yours."

"Now wait a minute...." Tyler's instinctive reaction was to accept the friendly puppy when she thrust it into his arms. The minute he drew it to his chest it wriggled happily and stretched up to lick the bottom of his chin.

"See?" Kara said, delighted. "Road Kill likes you."

"Yeah. I see that."

She watched his telling reaction to the little dog. It warmed her heart. Tyler Corbett might act antisocial toward her but he clearly had a way with animals. He couldn't be all bad. As a matter of fact, he looked thoroughly appealing as he stood there holding the fractious pup. His eyes sparkled with amusement, his mouth was curved into a charming smile, and the weariness seemed to have gone from his face.

It suddenly occurred to Kara that Tyler needed

the puppy as much as it needed him. He'd continued with his chores at the ranch and built a new way of life for himself after the loss of his wife, but apparently he didn't have anything in that life that needed his personal attention or his love the way Road Kill did.

Kara cleared the lump from her throat, then said, "I tell you what. How about keeping him just until his leg heals? I'm sure we can find a home for him then."

"I don't know...." Tyler glanced over his shoulder. "Buster doesn't usually like to share his turf."

Leaning to one side, Kara peered into the living room. A big, yellow Labrador retriever was lounging on the sofa as if it belonged to him. His muzzle was greying and his eyelids drooped, indicating he was pretty old. "Is that Buster? He doesn't look like he'd even bother getting up to sniff a puppy this small," Kara said. "Why don't we see?"

Tyler scowled down at her. "You're a determined woman, aren't you?"

"Yup." With that, she sidestepped and slipped past him. Approaching the sofa, she spoke quietly and extended her hand. "Hello, old boy. Would you like a playmate? Huh? Would you? I'll bet you would."

Buster lifted his broad head and nosed it beneath her hand to be petted. In the background, she heard Tyler say, "Well, I'll be."

"What's the matter?"

"Oh, nothing." He approached slowly, still holding Road Kill up out of the way in case the older dog objected. "I just haven't seen my dog take to anybody that fast before."

"I love animals," Kara said.

"Obviously they know it." He stepped closer. "Okay. Now what? Do we put this one down for Buster to sniff or do you want to hold him to introduce them?"

Relieved, Kara smiled up at him. "I take it this means you've decided to give it a try."

"It'll be temporary," Tyler reminded her. "I have plenty to do on the ranch. I don't have a lot of extra time to spend taking care of a puppy."

Nodding, she said, "I understand."

There was a strange, faraway quality to her voice which made him wonder what she really meant. "You do?"

"Oh, yes. I threw myself into my work after Alex died, too. It helps. Until I go home and have time to think. I suppose that's why I've taken in so many homeless animals. They give me company and keep my mind occupied."

Tyler was ashamed of himself. It didn't matter what kind of man Alex Shepherd had been, he'd still been Kara's husband. And she'd suffered the same kind of personal loss he had. Whether he liked it or not, they had a lot in common. No wonder he'd sensed an unexplainable camaraderie when he was in her presence. He'd been unfairly judging her for her husband's sins. In reality she was as much a victim of a meaningless tragedy as he was.

He bent to place the puppy in Kara's lap. "Here. You do the honors while I get us some coffee."

"I can't stay for coffee."

"Why not?" he asked pointedly.

"I have to get home and feed my animals." She shifted Road Kill so his nose faced Buster's and carefully let the two dogs sniff each other. Neither seemed upset about the encounter.

"One cup of coffee won't take long." He flashed her an amiable smile. "Humor me, okay?"

Kara didn't know what to say. The last thing she wanted to admit was that she was actually enjoying his company, in spite of the way he'd welcomed her at first. There was something soothing about being with Tyler. It was as if she no longer had to worry about doing or saying the wrong thing. He seemed to accept her as she was, not as she thought she should be, and the resulting feeling was strangely peaceful.

"All right. One cup," Kara said. "Lots of sugar."

Tyler chuckled. "You've heard about my coffee?"

"No. Why?" She was continuing to monitor the dogs but chanced a quick peek at him. He looked thoroughly amused.

"Dee used to tell me it would dissolve a spoon. Nobody's ever proved it, though."

"Let's hope I'm not the first," Kara said with a smile. "Maybe you'd better put some cream in it, too. Just to be on the safe side."

"Gotcha. Back in a minute."

She held Road Kill in her lap and continued to rhythmically stroke Buster's head after Tyler left the room. What was wrong with her? Didn't she have any sense? She hadn't come to the ranch to pay a social call or to befriend Tyler Corbett. She'd come to foist an injured dog on him. That was all. So why was she looking forward to a leisurely cup of coffee as if they were old friends?

Because he understands, she answered. And I understand how lonely he feels, too, even though I didn't share the same kind of wonderful love he once had.

Kara gazed down at the puppy, smiled and nodded her head. It looked like the Lord was in the process of healing a lot more than the little dog's broken leg. He was mending Tyler's broken heart, too.

She was glad to be able to help.

Chapter Four

"Here you go." Tyler held out one of the two mugs he'd just filled. "Lots of cream and sugar."

Kara carefully lowered the puppy to the rug at her feet and made sure he was comfortable before she reached to accept the steaming coffee. Cradling the hot mug in both hands, she took a whiff. "Mmm, this smells wonderful."

"Thanks." He perched on the arm of the sofa, purposely locating Buster between them as a buffer. "I have a question. Why were you the one who brought Road Kill to me? Why didn't you send your sister, instead? She's usually right in the thick of things."

"No kidding." Kara blew on the coffee, then took a cautious sip. Her eyes widened. "Wow. You weren't kidding when you described this stuff. I'll bet it keeps you awake all night if you drink much of it.''

"It's decaf," he countered. "Don't change the subject."

Eyes lowered, she sensed him studying her, waiting to see if she'd answer at all, let alone be truthful. She looked up as she said, "I came because Susan wanted me to do the honors, just in case."

"In case of what?" Tyler's brow furrowed.

"In case you got mad." Kara faced him squarely, surprised that she wasn't nearly as jumpy as usual, considering the gist of their conversation.

"What difference would that make to Susan?"

"Well..." Kara hesitated, taking time to chose her words carefully. "She didn't want to do anything that might adversely affect Mark's position with you, so she—"

Tyler got to his feet so quickly his coffee sloshed. He set the mug aside. "Whoa. Hold it a minute, lady. Do you mean to tell me that you and your sister think I'd be dumb enough to fire the best foreman I've ever had, just because his wife and sister-in-law happen to drive me nuts on a regular basis?"

"Well..."

He muttered under his breath. "You do have a pretty low opinion of me, don't you?"

"No. It's not like that at all," Kara insisted. Their pleasant conversation had deteriorated so rapidly she felt she'd better try to say or do something that would reverse the negative trend, if only for Susan's sake. Rising, she cautiously stepped over the resting pup.

Tyler folded his arms across his chest and remained resolute as she approached. "Oh? Then how is it?"

"It's a long story." Kara willed him to understand and hoped she wasn't making a mistake by confiding in him. "Susan and I come from a wonderful family, really we do. It's just that our father had a pretty short temper, sometimes. He yelled a lot. Especially when I was a teen. Susan used to intervene on my behalf all the time."

Tyler's frown deepened. "What's that got to do with me?"

"Nothing, directly. But we've discussed it more than once and decided that may be the reason she and I tend to avoid unpleasant confrontations whenever possible."

"I see."

Kara could tell by the leery look in his eyes and his standoffish posture that he didn't see a thing. That didn't surprise her. None of her friends had ever believed that her dad could be a monster when he lost his temper, either. His company-face was unblemished. Outsiders had never seen him behave irrationally or heard him shout at his family until he was hoarse, so why should they believe the wild tales of an uptight teenager?

And then, heaven help her, she'd married a man just like him. She'd been searching for someone who was kind and gentle, who loved animals as much as she did, and she'd been totally fooled into thinking Alex Shepherd was the perfect choice. She shivered. What irony.

Taking a deep, settling breath Kara managed a nonchalant smile as she turned her back on Tyler and started for the door. "Well, thanks for the coffee. I have to be going."

He opened his mouth to ask her to stay longer, then changed his mind. Having a normal chat with this woman was impossible. Every time he decided she was intrinsically antisocial, she came up with some revealing tidbit that tugged at his heart so strongly he was tempted to take her in his arms and offer comfort.

His breath caught. Now *that* would be a mistake to end all mistakes. Half the time, Kara was as prickly as a porcupine. Yet she could also be as gentle, as vulnerable, as a doe. With his luck, he'd give in and decide to hug her just about the time she stuck her quills up!

Following her to the door, he found he was smiling at the analogy.

Kara caught him grinning. "What's so funny?"

"Nothing. I was just thinking."

"About me?"

"Sort of."

"I don't want to know more, do I?" she asked wisely.

"Probably not."

"I didn't think so." She extended her hand. "Thanks for agreeing to take Roady. He really is a sweet-natured little guy. I'm sure he and Buster will get along fine."

Instead of shaking her hand, Tyler opened the door and stood back. "I'm only keeping the dog until he's healed up."

"Of course." Kara felt like cheering! By the time she got around to removing the cast, Road Kill would be so much a part of Tyler Corbett's life he'd beg her to let the puppy stay. Naturally, she'd have to give in and allow it.

Stifling a triumphant smile, she hurried to her car, climbed in and drove away. Things were going to work out fine as long as Susan didn't interfere and try to "help." The Corbett ranch was the perfect place for a rambunctious pup, and having a canine companion might give old Buster a new lease on life, too.

Kara's smile turned wistful. What a lovely, tender scene she'd beheld when she'd first entered Tyler's living room. The elderly, yellow Lab was as much a permanent fixture in the casually furnished ranch house as the soft, leather sofa he'd claimed as his own. Clearly, he was a well-loved member of the family.

Tears began to cloud her vision. Disgusted, she blinked them back. What was the matter with her?

The mercy mission had gone well. Roady had a good home with a loving man who'd watch over him and care about him. So why get emotional now? *Why, indeed?*

Suddenly, Kara realized what was bothering her. The concept wasn't rational, nor could she explain what had caused her to make such a ridiculous comparison. Only one thing was certain. In spite of her aversion to marriage and commitment, she envied the *dogs.* They'd found unconditional love. And someone they could always trust.

It didn't matter that their master was Tyler Corbett. The important thing was they truly belonged.

For the first time in months, Kara dreaded Sunday. She wasn't about to let anything keep her out of church, she just wasn't keen on running into Tyler there. To be on the safe side, she'd spent the two days since her visit to his ranch rehearsing a series of nonchalant comments to use in case they happened to come face-to-face.

Knowing that the Corbetts and their friends usually sat together in the third and fourth rows, Kara took a seat near the rear of the old stone church, greeting fellow worshipers with a demure smile.

This was the church she'd attended before her marriage. Afterward, Alex had insisted they didn't need to worship in a small, country church that didn't offer him much opportunity to further his practice by impressing wealthy, local ranchers with his intellect and supposed piety. Kara never had been able to make him understand how at home and peaceful she felt when she sat quietly in that little church and allowed the Lord to fill her heart with His love. She sighed. Words couldn't describe how good it felt to be back.

The day had promised to be warm so she'd wound her long hair into a twist and fastened it up with a large, tortoiseshell clip that matched the muted colors of her softly draped, rayon print dress. She was smoothing her skirt when all of a sudden her sense of peace vanished.

Wisps of hair on the back of her neck tickled, prickled and would have stood on end if they hadn't been so long. She tensed. It wasn't necessary to look over her shoulder to know what was wrong. Tyler Corbett had arrived. She could feel his presence.

The broad-shouldered man passed right by Kara as he made his way forward, down the center aisle. On his arm was a slim, blond-haired lady. Kara raised one eyebrow. *Well, well. And who might this be?* She wasn't surprised that she didn't recognize the woman. Since she'd only recently begun attending this church again, there were many people she didn't know, or faces she couldn't place.

What did bother Kara, however, was the unexpected twinge of jealousy when Tyler and his companion had walked by. What a silly response! Why should she care who he was with?

Susan slid into the pew next to her and nudged her gently. "Scoot over, will you? Mark's coming as soon as he parks the car. I was afraid we'd be late so I had him let me off at the door. One of the horses picked last night to foal and we were up half the night."

"Why didn't you call me?" Kara whispered. "You know I'd have come out to help."

Susan made a face. "I thought of that. Mark said no. It seems Tyler wasn't too pleased when you dropped by the other day."

"That's *your* fault." Kara wasn't about to back down. "You talked me into doing it. I wanted you to take the puppy to him in the first place."

"I know. My mistake." She shielded her mouth with one cupped hand and leaned closer. "What did you say to the man, anyway? Mark says he's been a real pill ever since you were out there."

Shrugging, Kara was at a loss. "I don't know. We just talked. Made polite conversation. The usual." She remembered her confession about their father's bad temper but could see no connection between that and Tyler's mood. "He seemed okay when I left." A sly smile lit her face. "Of course, I did foist an injured dog on him. Maybe that's what's bothering him."

"Maybe." Susan slid closer as her husband

joined them. "And maybe he's just naturally mean-spirited."

"Oh, I don't think so," Kara said quickly. She noticed a look of smug satisfaction come over her sister and easily anticipated her thoughts. "Don't start with me again about needing a husband," she warned. "Don't even start."

Susan almost managed to look innocent. "Who? Me? I didn't say a word."

"No, but I know what you were thinking. I told you, I have no interest in *any* man, least of all Tyler Corbett. Besides, he's got a special lady friend. Look. Third row. Second from the left."

Leaning sideways, the elder sister peered between the heads of other worshipers until she spotted her quarry. "Aha. I do see. How interesting that you noticed."

"The man walked right by me. I couldn't help but see him. Now, will you please leave me alone?"

"Till the service is over," Susan said. "Then you and I are going to find Mr. Corbett so I can properly introduce you to his lady friend."

"It won't be necessary to go to..." Kara began.

Susan pointed to the front of the sanctuary. "Shush. They're starting. I can't hear a thing when you're talking."

Disgusted, Kara closed her mouth. Her mind, however, refused to be quieted. No way was she going to permit her sister to drag her into another unnecessary discussion with Tyler Corbett. Especially since he'd brought a female companion to church!

Not that she cared one way or the other, Kara insisted. He was widowed. He was entitled to find somebody else to fill the void in his life.

On the other hand, the emptiness Alex had left in *her* life was a blessing. Yes, she sometimes felt guilty for thinking like that. There were even times when she missed the man she thought she'd married. But truth was truth. Alex had been a beguiling, blasphemous hypocrite with a volatile temper. It was only a matter of time before he'd have stepped over the line and done something truly horrendous—to her or to someone else. Maybe both.

She'd never wished him harm in a literal sense. She'd simply been frightened and unsure of what to do when he'd gotten drunk, flown into a rage and stormed out of the house for the last time. The decision to drive away had been his. Investigators had assured her that the fatal, single-car crash was no one else's fault. Alex had made many wrong choices. Ultimately, one of them had led to his death.

All she had to do was accept what had happened and get on with her life. Thank God she was finally healing; finally beginning to feel normal again.

Even if being normal meant she was beginning to notice a good-looking, appealing man when she saw one? Kara asked herself. She nodded. *Oh, yes.* She could handle her emotions. Thanks to Alex, she was no innocent, naive girl. Not anymore.

The Sunday morning church service was over far too soon to suit Kara. She gathered up her purse and bible, intending to make a quick exit as the rest of the congregation began to file out of the sanctuary.

Susan grabbed her arm. "Hey! Not so fast. Come with me. I'm going to introduce you to somebody special. Remember?"

"Sorry. I don't have the time. I have to stop at the grocery store on my way home, then drop by the hospital to check on the sheltie we took in on Friday."

"And don't forget, you have to wash your hair, too." Susan grinned knowingly.

"What?" Kara patted the twist at the back of her head to make sure it was still neatly in place. "What are you talking about?"

"Just being a good sister and providing extra excuses, in case you run out."

"Very funny." Kara tried to sidle past. The aisle was blocked. Short of being impolite and shoving somebody out of the way, she was temporarily trapped.

Taking advantage, Susan grabbed her by the hand and tugged her backward until they were once again standing between the two rows of padded pews where they'd been seated.

Only five feet two inches tall, Kara wasn't able to see over people's heads as well as her sister could. She strained on tiptoe, checking every glimpse of a dark-blue suit in the crowd, hoping that Tyler wasn't going to pass by before she could make a graceful exit.

It took her only a few seconds to realize she wasn't going to get her wish. She lifted her chin proudly and smiled as Tyler and his well-dressed companion inched past.

Behind her, Susan squealed so boisterously that dozens of people stopped to stare. "Louise Tate! It is you! I'm so glad to see you decided to come today. Welcome!" She leaned around Kara and extended her hand, grinning widely when the woman took it. "This is my sister, Kara."

Louise smiled pleasantly. "How nice to finally get to meet you. Susan has told me a lot about you."

Uh-oh. Kara couldn't help but smile in response to the woman's happy glow and the elfin look in her twinkling blue eyes. The only thing that amazed her was Louise's evident age. It looked as if Tyler preferred older women. *Much* older women. With ash-blond hair that hinted at grey.

"Louise is Deanne's mother. You know…Tyler's wife. I mean late wife." Susan blushed. "Oh, dear. I'm sorry. I shouldn't have put it that way."

Louise patted her on the arm. "Nonsense. We all want to remember Deanne. She was a lovely girl. I'm proud to have had her for a daughter. It bothers me when people avoid mentioning her because they think it will hurt me."

Worried about how Tyler might be affected by the candid conversation, Kara glanced up at him, expecting the worst. Instead, she found him staring at her as if he hadn't heard a word anyone had said. Their gazes met. Held for an instant too long. She blinked to break the silent bond and looked over at Susan, hoping she hadn't noticed. She obviously had.

"My sister's a widow, too," Susan volunteered, her voice brisk and enthusiastic, "but I guess I told you that already, didn't I?"

"Yes, you did," the older woman said. She smiled sweetly at Kara. "I hope I'm not speaking out of turn, dear. At my age it's a lot easier to get away with saying what I really think." She punctuated her statement with a soft chuckle. "I must tell you, now that I've met you, I'm surprised you're still single."

Kara opened her mouth to express her opposing point of view.

Susan cut her off before she got started. "She says she likes being on her own. I sure wouldn't. I don't know how I'd manage if I didn't have my Mark to come home to every night."

"I know exactly what you mean," Louise agreed. "I've outlived two wonderful husbands. If the right man came into my life right now, I'd marry again in a heartbeat."

Pointed comments were flying back and forth between Susan and Louise so rapidly, Kara felt like a spectator at a tennis match. She rolled her eyes in disbelief and looked up at Tyler for validation of her cynical attitude.

He nodded in agreement. Kara relaxed and smiled at him, secure in the knowledge that she could do so without giving him the wrong impression.

His eyebrows arched comically, one corner of his mouth lifting in a wry smile, as he took his mother-in-law's arm. "Come on, Louise. I'll treat you to lunch and we'll brainstorm about finding you another husband. How's that?"

"Well, I—" She was hustled away before she could finish the sentence.

When Tyler glanced back over his shoulder, Kara mouthed a silent, "Thank you."

He replied with an equally silent, "You're welcome," and gifted her with a heartwarming smile.

Kara felt the effects of that stunning smile all the way from the top of her head to her toes. A shiver skittered up her spine. On its heels was a warm glow.

Taken aback, she waved her church bulletin like

a fan to cool her suddenly flushed cheeks. "Whew!"

A wide, satisfied grin split Susan's face. "What's the matter? Too hot for you?"

"It is warm in here," Kara offered, still fanning.

Susan snickered. "Hah! The air temperature has nothing to do with your being so hot under the collar, and you know it."

"Don't be silly."

"I'm not the one being silly." Susan bent to pick up her purse and bible. She was still grinning broadly as she waved goodbye to Kara with a blithe, "See you tomorrow."

Chapter Five

The veterinary office was finally empty, the last client on his way home. Exhausted, Kara sank into the chair behind the front counter, propped her feet up and sighed. "Boy, I don't know what's the matter with me lately."

Concerned, her sister leaned against the filing cabinet. "Are you sick?"

"No. It's not that. I'm…well…distracted. Sort of befuddled. I have been all week. It's like I have spring fever or something, and it's wearing me to a frazzle."

"I wasn't going to mention it, but you have been acting kind of *out to lunch,* lately. And I'm not talking about food." She laughed lightly. "Course, I shouldn't talk. I'm the one who shaved Mrs. Pettibone's tomcat's tummy so you could spay him!"

"That was so funny," Kara agreed with a chuckle. "You should have seen the look on your face when you realized what you'd done."

"It wasn't entirely my fault, you know. His name's Miss Priss."

"Not anymore. Mrs. Pettibone was so shocked to learn he was a boy that she decided to change his name. I think she finally settled on Rufus." Kara paused. "Which reminds me, how's Road Kill?"

"A cat named Rufus reminds you of Road Kill? That's a stretch of the imagination."

"He's been on my mind lately."

"Are we talking about the *dog,* here?"

"Of course we are." Kara made a silly face.

Susan's eyes glimmered with mischief. "And you have no interest in how Tyler is?"

"He's all right, isn't he?"

"Aha!" Susan was jubilant. "I knew you were thinking of him all along."

"What if I was? I'm still worried you and Mark will get into trouble with him because of me."

"Hey, don't worry about us. We're fine. Mark got a raise and he loves his job, so things couldn't be better." She studied her younger sister perceptively. "Except that I hate to see you sitting home all alone, night after night."

Kara's "Hah!" was loud, abrupt. "I live with four dogs, six cats, and keep a spoiled rotten, retired carriage horse in my side pasture. I'd hardly call that being alone."

"Okay. Besides the Kara Shepherd Home for Antique Animals, what do you have to look forward to?"

"Peace and quiet, for one."

"As opposed to an interesting human companion who cares about you? I'd hardly call that a fair trade."

"Well, I would," Kara insisted.

"Maybe." Susan gave her a friendly pat on the back. "But it's really none of my business so let's change the subject. What are you doing for dinner Saturday night?"

Kara scowled up at her. "I thought we were changing the subject."

"We are. I've got a really delicious-looking pork roast in the fridge. I thought I'd stick it on the rotisserie. Cook it real slow. Only it's way too big for just Mark and me to eat all by ourselves."

"You could serve it two days in a row."

Susan shook her head. "I could. Or I could ask my favorite sister to share it with us. That is, if she isn't too stubborn to admit she gets lonesome once in a while."

"Okay. Once in a while I suppose I do. But remember, living by myself is my choice." She smiled to assure Susan she wasn't upset. "So, what can I bring?"

"Yourself," Susan said enthusiastically. "We'll have a great time. You'll see. I can hardly wait!"

Eyeing her suspiciously, Kara wondered why anyone would be so excited about having a sibling over for dinner. Especially since it wasn't that rare an occasion. She decided to ask. "Why is it I'm getting the idea you're way too happy about all this?"

"I'm just a basically cheerful person. You used to be, too, before—" Looking penitent, Susan said, "Sorry."

"Hey, don't be. I know I've changed since we were kids. Everybody has to grow up sometime." She smiled and pointed. "Even you."

"Not me," Susan countered. "I plan to stay a big kid all my life. It's more fun that way."

Kara's smile faded. *Fun* was a concept she'd put aside for self-preservation when she'd realized what kind of man her husband really was. He hadn't liked the sound of her normal laugh; said it was too shrill, too loud. So to keep the peace, she'd minimized it. During the course of her marriage she'd squelched her good humor so often she'd almost forgotten how to let go; how to have ordinary fun the way Susan did, especially when she and Mark were together.

That was one reason Kara didn't like to spend too much time in their company. It hurt to see what a good marriage could be like and to know how rare it was.

What a blessing it would have been to find that kind of husband, she thought wistfully. To have the kind of perfect partnership Susan and Mark shared. The same kind that Tyler Corbett had once had with his beloved Deanne.

* * *

"I don't know why she's so intent on putting on such a big spread," Mark said, dusting off his hands and facing his boss. "All I know is, when my wife gets a bee in her bonnet, it's best to let her have her way." He flashed a wide grin. "You don't mind, do you?"

Tyler shrugged. "No. I'm flattered. What time shall I come?"

"I don't know. We usually eat around six. Just wander over an hour or so before that and you can help me light the barbecue. Susan's been cooking a roast on the electric rotisserie all day but I still have corn on the cob and taters to do on the grill."

"Sounds delicious. Can I bring anything?"

"Nope. As long as you show up and help me keep peace in my family, I'll be satisfied. Susan left it up to me to invite you and I got the idea she wasn't going to take it kindly if I didn't succeed."

Tyler chuckled. He took his hat off and raked his fingers through his hair, combing it back. "She sure is something when she makes up her mind, that's a fact. Has she always been so stubborn?"

"Far as I know. She's been that way as long as I've known her. Ever since she was sixteen."

"Is Kara older or younger?" Tyler asked.

"Younger. Susan turned thirty in March—only don't you dare let on I told you or I'll be in the doghouse for sure. Kara's twenty-six."

Tyler made a skeptical sound low in his throat. "You could have fooled me."

"I know what you mean. Kara's so serious all the time, it makes her seem older."

"Was she always like that?"

Mark shrugged. "I'm not sure. I was eighteen when I first met Kara. And so in love with Susan I couldn't see straight. I'm afraid I didn't pay much attention to her baby sister." He grew thoughtful. "Seems to me she was always pretty studious, though. Had her nose buried in a book most of the time."

"What about their parents?" Tyler asked, remembering Kara's confession. "Were they strict?"

"Their father was," Mark said without hesitation. "I used to hear him ranting and raving some nights when I was sitting out on the porch with Susie. She never seemed to take him seriously but I sure did. Believe me, I *always* got her home before her curfew."

Tyler had to know more. "Is he still living?"

"Nope. Flew into a rage one day and had a stroke. He didn't live long after that. Susan said his heart gave out." Mark snorted wryly. "If you ask me, he didn't have one."

"That must have been hard on the sisters."

"It was." He paused to recall. "They both flew back to Illinois for the funeral. So did I. Alex and Kara had been married about a year by then. He never bothered to show up. I thought that was kinda strange."

"Must have made it worse for her," Tyler ventured.

"You'd think so. But if I remember right, I never heard her mention his name the whole time we were at her mother's."

"Not even once?"

"Nope. Well, I'd better go get that corn."

Tyler didn't pay much attention. He was thinking about Kara and visualizing her as a sensitive child who'd buried herself in her studies to escape rancor in the home, while her sister had merely shrugged off the same situation and hadn't let it bother her. Too bad they couldn't have both been immune the way Susan was.

He quickly convinced himself it wasn't his problem. He didn't want to know what made Kara Shepherd tick. Or what experiences, good or bad, had formed her into the person she was today.

Except that she intrigued him, he admitted ruefully. There was something about her that drew him, caused his normally staid emotions to threaten to run amok when she looked at him with those soft, doe eyes of hers. It was almost as if he couldn't bring himself to look away, once their gazes met.

You're a fool to look at another woman in the first place, he told himself. You had the best. You had Deanne. She was one of a kind.

Tyler nodded slowly, pensively. His days had been blessed beyond imagination by his marriage. He firmly believed that a perfect love only came along once in a lifetime. In spite of what his former mother-in-law kept insisting about finding another husband for herself, he was certain his personal quota of miracles had been used up. That was enough to convince him he'd never court anyone else. Ever.

When Kara's winsome face popped into his consciousness unbidden and he muttered in disgust, *"Especially* not her," he was very thankful Mark wasn't there to hear him.

Kara arrived at Susan's just in time to help her set the dining room table.

"We were going to eat in the yard but the bugs have been terrible," Susan said. "Mark insists it's because last winter was too mild."

"Probably. We need a long, cold spell to kill off a lot of the worst pests. Of course, there is a plus side. We'll sell a lot more flea and tick killer."

"Good point." Susan grinned. "Hey, maybe we could breed the little critters and make even more money!"

Kara huffed in mock derision. "This is Arkansas, dear heart. Nobody has to try to breed insects here. They just appear in droves the minute the weather gets the tiniest bit warm. I don't know what I'd do without the Purple Martins that nest out at my place."

"Eating mosquitoes, you mean?"

"Those, and every other flying insect they can

catch on the wing. I must have twenty pairs of martins in my birdhouses so far this year and they're singing like wild canaries to attract mates. It's wonderful. I wake up to a concert every morning.''

Susan giggled. "I wake up to Mark's snoring."

"Well, to each his own. I prefer my birds," Kara teased. "They don't make funny noises. And they always clean up after themselves."

"But they don't keep your feet warm at night."

"I have an electric blanket." She made a face. "If it stops working, I can buy another one."

A pleasant voice coming from behind her made Kara jump. "Buy another one what?" Louise Tate asked.

Kara whirled. "Oh! Hello. You startled me." She smiled for Louise's benefit, then shot a questioning glance at Susan.

"I take it you didn't know I was coming," the older woman observed. "I hope you don't mind."

"No, of course not. It's nice to see you again."

Susan smiled broadly and reached past Kara for the bowl Louise was carrying. "Oooh, fruit salad. How delicious."

"I didn't want to come empty-handed," she said. "If you don't want to serve it tonight, you and Mark can always have it later, when we're all gone."

We? All? Kara was beginning to have serious misgivings about the forthcoming evening. She had a bad feeling that Louise might be only the first of the surprises her sister had in store.

Before she could ask, Mark burst in the back door, still dusty from work. "Sorry, ladies," he said in passing. "I got delayed. I'll go grab a quick shower and be right back." He stopped in the hallway and stuck his head back through the door to the kitchen where Susan, Louise and Kara stood. "If Ty gets here before I'm done cleaning up, ask him to go ahead and light the barbecue, will you?"

Kara's mouth dropped open. She wheeled to face her sister. "Susan…"

"Hey, it's a big roast," she countered. "No sense in letting it go to waste. Besides, there's nothing wrong with trying to make points with the boss." She smiled sweetly. "I kiss up to mine all the time."

Kara's, "Oh, save me!" practically rattled the windows. She quickly excused herself, spun on her heel and headed for the door. Of all the ridiculous tricks Susan had pulled, this one took the prize.

Jerking open the screen, Kara plunged outside, ran down the steps onto the lawn and nearly collided with Tyler Corbett.

He put out his arms to catch her. It wasn't necessary. She managed to skid to a stop and regain her balance without stumbling, then step back out of reach.

Filled with annoyance, she put her fists on her hips, braced herself and stared up at him. It was easy to see he was as shocked to see her as she'd been to learn that he was also invited to dinner.

Kara nodded toward the house. "I wouldn't go in there if I were you."

"Why not?" Scowling, Tyler stood his ground.

"Because there's apparently a plot brewing. I don't know why I'm surprised. My sister's done this kind of thing before."

"Done what?"

"Gotten it into her head that I'm desperate for a husband and tried to hurry things along. I hate to tell you this, but I think she's picked you for the job." She grimaced. "Louise is in the house, too. I suspect a conspiracy."

His eyes widened. "Dee's mother? Why would she be involved?"

"I don't have a clue. All I know is she seemed to know you were coming and didn't act a bit surprised to find me in the kitchen with Susan when she arrived a few minutes ago."

Tyler was slowly, pensively shaking his head. "I suppose you could be right. Louise has been repeating her marital history a lot lately. I figured she was getting senile. Now that I think about it, she may have been using those stories to try to get me to consider finding another wife." He looked directly into Kara's eyes as he added, "That will never happen. Deanne was one of a kind."

Kara began to relax. Taking a deep breath, she released it as a relieved sigh. "I know what you mean. After Alex, I swear I'll never get married again."

"Why can't they just leave us alone?" Tyler sounded melancholy.

"I don't know. Probably because they care about us too much." She was starting to get an idea and didn't want to discuss it where they could be overheard. "Come on. Let's take a little walk."

He eyed her with suspicion as she urged him away from the house. "Why?"

"Because I know how we can get everybody to relax and leave us alone," she said brightly. "It's brilliant. And plausible. I've used similar tricks to get Susan to back off, before. It'll serve them right if they swallow the whole charade, hook, line and sinker."

"We're fishing?" Tyler teased. He was beginning to suspect where Kara's mind was going and couldn't help being amused by her enthusiasm.

"No, we're bamboozling. We're going to make them think we're a couple! We'll have to work out the beginning of our pretend relationship, of course. It has to look natural or we won't fool anybody. That'll be the hardest part."

"You're crazy. They'll never buy it."

"Sure they will. It'll be easy, especially if we throw in a suitable lovers' quarrel every once in a while." She grinned up at him. "How about it? Think you can argue with me convincingly?"

"I think we can manage that part all right," he said hesitantly. "The friendly stuff may be tougher."

"Not once we get used to it. Lots of couples have rotten home lives and still manage to present a loving image when they're out in public."

"That's not a very comforting picture."

Kara agreed. "No. But it does prove my plan is doable. What do you say? Shall we try it?"

"I'm not sure. Suppose Susan doesn't fall for the same trick again? And what about Louise?"

"If it doesn't fool them, then we're right back where we started. We won't have lost a thing." Kara's eyebrows arched. "But if the plan *works,* we can string them along for months, maybe even years, till we either get tired of acting the part or you meet somebody else and decide to move on."

Laying her hand on his arm she sobered. "I know what's bothering you. It's deceitful. That part bothers me, too. If our friends were trying to manipulate us like this, we could just tell them off. But Louise and Susan are family. We can't disown them just because they're trying to do us a favor, even when they're wrong."

Tyler looked down at where her warm hand rested on his forearm. If he wasn't so positive he'd never be able to replace Deanne, he'd never agree to such a bizarre plan. If it worked, however, there could be added benefits that Kara hadn't mentioned. "Okay. I'll do it. But only because I think it will demonstrate to Louise and everybody else that I am *not* going to change my mind."

"Ditto." Kara extended her hand. "Shake on it?"

He complied, then quickly released her and stepped back, sliding his fingers into the back pockets of his jeans. "Okay. You're the brains of this outfit. How do we get started?"

She smoothed the hem of her T-shirt over her hips while she gave her imagination free rein. "Well, you could always kiss me and then I could slap your face."

"Why would I *kiss* you?" Flushing, he realized his initial astonishment at the suggestion had made him sound too hostile. "I mean, doesn't that seem too quick?"

She subdued her bruised pride and managed a cynical smile. "Hmmm. You're right. So why don't we just wing it? We've already decided we're going to have a few lovers' quarrels. I think you'll do just fine at that kind of scene without a script."

Tyler didn't miss the extra dollop of cloying sweetness in her voice—or the smug look on her face. "Cute. Sounds to me like you won't need one, either."

"See? You're starting to appreciate my quick wit already. Come on." Kara started back to the house. "I'll go in the kitchen door. You'd better wait a few minutes and use the front so we don't look like we're together."

"I thought that was the idea."

"Not yet. That's too easy. They'll never buy it if we give in too willingly."

He slowed his pace. "Okay. I suppose you're right. You go on back. I'll follow in a few minutes."

"Right." Suddenly nervous, she paused and smoothed her pale-blue top again. "Do I look okay?"

He wanted to tell her she looked wonderful. The shirt fit her nicely, without being too tight the way some women wore them, and her jeans were so right for her they may as well have been tailored to her precise measurements.

"You'll do," he said dryly. "You're not auditioning for *Macbeth*, you know."

Kara giggled. "I feel like it."

"Scared?" Tyler stepped closer to speak in confidence. They were barely fifty feet from Mark and Susan's. The sun was low in the west, the ranch as quiet as it ever got, and he didn't want their conversation accidentally overheard.

"A little," she said softly. "I know it's crazy but it really bothers me to think of deceiving Susan. She's always there for me when I need her. I love her a lot."

"We don't have to go ahead with this, you know. It's not too late to change your mind." Stepping closer, Tyler waited for her final decision.

Kara's words were so soft he could barely hear them. He rested his hands lightly on her shoulders and leaned down, inclining his head to one side. "What did you say?"

She was about to repeat, "I know," when she saw

a flash of movement past Tyler's shoulder. It was Mark. And he was staring right at them!

Before Kara could warn Tyler or step away from him, Mark let out a hoot of surprise, then bolted for the house.

Tyler spun around. "What was that?"

"I think it was the opening of act I, scene 1," she said, her heart racing, her cheeks turning crimson. "My brother-in-law just caught us out behind the barn."

Mark shot through the door and shouted, "Hey! You won't believe what I just saw!"

Susan and Louise froze where they stood. Susan finally found her voice enough to ask, "What?"

"Kara and Tyler."

"So?"

"Together!" he added, pointing. "Out there."

"Were they killing each other?" Susan was rapidly drying her hands, preparing to go to Kara's rescue.

Mark snickered. "That sure wasn't what it looked like to me. I didn't stand around and stare but I'd swear they were pretty friendly."

Louise let out the breath she'd been holding. "Whew. That's a relief."

"I'll believe it when I see it." Susan was already headed for the door. She grabbed a handful of her husband's shirt in passing and tugged him along behind. "Show me."

* * *

Tyler was having trouble dealing with the unacceptable awareness he'd felt when he'd made the mistake of innocently touching Kara's shoulders. He told himself he should have already learned the folly of doing anything like that. It had happened for the first time when she'd asked him to hold back her hair while she'd doctored the pup's leg. This time was worse. This time, he'd had no reasonable excuse for his actions.

"What do we do now?" Kara whispered.

"Don't ask me. I suppose we could claim we were quarreling, like we'd planned."

"Even *I* wouldn't believe that one, and this story is my invention."

"Well, what then?"

She pulled a face. "I don't know. Maybe we can—"

Just then, Tyler saw everyone else rush out of the house. Mark was pointing.

"Go to Plan B." Tyler finished her sentence with a self-deprecating smirk, grabbed Kara and pulled her into a full embrace. As he bent to kiss her, he whispered a warning against her lips. "Hang on. This won't hurt a bit."

The moment he took her in his arms, Kara's brain curled into a useless knot and ceased rational function. The touch of his lips only added to the turmoil. She wrapped her arms around Tyler's neck and held tight as he lifted her off the ground. If this was his idea of a make-believe kiss, she was glad he'd never give her a real one! It might be so wonderful she'd die from its sweetness.

Tyler released her almost immediately, although it seemed as if eons had passed while their lips were pressed together. Guilt assailed him. He'd pledged himself to Deanne for eternity, yet he'd savored the taste, the touch of Kara's kiss. That was wrong. It had to be.

He started to back off.

Kara blinked repeatedly, trying to focus her thoughts. She wasn't scared. She wasn't anything. Her brain was drawing a complete blank, leaving her feeling about as resourceful as a bowl of cold, week-old grits.

When Tyler looked down at her and gazed silently into her eyes, she could hardly breathe. "What—what did you do *that* for?"

"We have an audience. Plan B. Remember?"

Kara remembered all right. She also remembered exactly what she was supposed to do in return. "Well, you started it," she muttered. "I guess I can finish it."

Drawing back, she slapped his face so hard her palm stung, spun on her heel and stalked away.

Chapter Six

Kara stormed past her openmouthed sister and the others and reentered the kitchen, slamming the screen door behind her. If the idiotic plan to pretend she was interested in Tyler hadn't been her own, she'd have had someone else to blame. But there was no way to disclaim accountability. There was nothing left to do but try to carry out the entire plan.

Susan and Louise followed her inside a few minutes later. Kara's cheeks were still flaming, her eyes flashing, when she whirled to face the other women and peered past them. "Where's Mark?"

"Outside, attacking the grill so we can roast the corn," Susan said simply.

"And Mr. Corbett?"

"Outside." Susan half smiled. "Or were you asking if Mark was attacking him, too?"

"Very funny." Kara didn't have to act the part of a flustered woman. She was truly upset about what had just occurred between her and Tyler. The worst part was she could still feel the touch of his lips, still sense his nearness, still taste his kiss.

"Actually, I thought it *was* pretty funny," Susan replied. "You should have seen the look on your face afterward."

"I don't want to discuss it. And I don't appreciate what you tried to do tonight." She focused on her sister. "I'm never going to be able to trust you again."

Susan held up her hands in mock surrender. "Hey. I didn't tell him to kiss you. And I certainly didn't make you kiss him back." She chuckled quietly and smiled over at Louise. "It didn't look to me like Kara minded much. Did it to you?"

"No, I can't say it did," Louise drawled. "As a matter of fact, I'm not sure Tyler started it. It seemed to me that Kara was as much a party to what took place as he was."

"I was not!"

Susan cocked her head quizzically as she asked, "Do you mean to tell us the man knocked you out and dragged you off behind the barn so he could ravish you?"

"No. Of course not." Resolute, Kara faced her sister, hands on her hips, jaw clenched.

"So, you went with him all by yourself, right?"

"Yes, but…"

"Aha. I thought so. I couldn't see you letting any

man take advantage of you, if you didn't want him to.''

That's true, now that Alex is gone, Kara thought. I am much stronger willed than I used to be. She refused to be swayed. "We were just talking. That's all."

"About what?"

The knowing look in Susan's eyes told Kara her ruse was working, in spite of the plan getting off to a rocky start. She supposed that was better than failure, even though it had meant she'd learned something disturbing about herself. And about her vulnerability…or what was left of it.

Whether she liked it or not, she was attracted to Tyler Corbett, at least on a physical level. Of course, she'd never let him guess that was the case. Their scheme would still work. All she had to do was keep him from demonstrating any more of his romantic tendencies and all would be well.

Kara let herself smile as if she were hiding a delicious secret, then said, "Tyler and I were talking. That's all you need to know, nosy."

A triumphant expression bloomed on Susan's face. She glanced over at Louise, clearly pleased with herself.

Kara's troubled conscience did a back flip and landed as a heavy lump of guilt in her chest. She averted her gaze. There were two ways to get her meddlesome yet devoted sister to leave her love life alone. One was the way she'd chosen; a sham romance with a man who could be trusted to keep a confidence and not misunderstand her motives. The second was to reveal the truth about her horrible marriage to Alex so Susan would understand why choosing another husband was not something Kara would ever consider.

In any fair contest the truth should prevail, she knew. And maybe someday she'd find the courage to confide in her sister. But not now. Not yet.

The urge to unburden herself faded. Forcing a smile, Kara reached for a paring knife. "Okay. Let's get back to work, here. Which do you want me to fix, the green salad or the potatoes?"

Without speaking, Tyler followed Mark to the patio and watched him light the barbecue grill. He felt like he ought to say something—anything—that would explain why he'd been kissing Kara. He snorted in self-derision. If *he* knew why he'd done it, he'd have a lot better chance of explaining the whole thing to someone else.

It had been a spur-of-the-moment decision. One he'd been regretting ever since he'd acted upon it. In retrospect, he realized he'd gathered her so close he'd even lifted her feet off the ground. Considering how short she was compared to Deanne, he supposed his reactions had been instinctive. *And stupid*, he added. What must poor Kara think of him?

His hand lifted to touch his still-tingling cheek.

Poor Kara, indeed. For a little gal she sure packed a big wallop.

Mark was watching him and chuckling softly. "Sorry. If I'd known you were going to try to kiss my sister-in-law, I'd have warned you. She's not the most approachable woman in the world."

"No kidding." Tyler shook his head, remembering. "I don't think I'll try that again."

"Oh, I wouldn't give up on her too soon. She's one smart lady. Once she sees you're not just stringing her along, she should come around." He paused, studying Tyler. "I'd hate to be the guy who messes up her life, though."

"Why? Do you think she'd deck him?"

"No," Mark said soberly. "But I'd have to."

It was crowded in the dining room when everyone gathered around the small, oak table for dinner.

Kara had judiciously avoided making eye contact with Tyler when he and Mark had come inside bearing their contributions to the meal, hot off the grill.

She'd already made up her mind she was *not* going to sit next to Tyler. Thankfully, he seemed bent on sidestepping any additional contact with her, too.

Planning ahead, Kara put her newly filled iced tea glass by the place setting between Louise's and Susan's. Then she waited for one or the other of them to try to maneuver her next to Tyler, instead. Neither did.

With a relieved sigh and prayerful thanks to her

heavenly Father for the respite, she plopped into her chair, exhausted. It seemed to take a lot more energy to carry on a charade than it did to simply live one's life in a forthright manner. At least that was the way it worked for her. She wondered absently if Tyler'd felt the same weariness after he'd kissed her.

The thought of that kiss, *his* kiss, instantly made her heart rate speed up, her hands tremble. Kara held motionless for a moment, then chanced a look at the others. Did her embarrassing reaction to her errant thoughts show? Was she making a worse fool of herself than she already had?

Thankfully, no one was paying the least attention to her. Mark was carving the roast while he and Louise discussed the merits of rotisserie cooking. Susan was emerging from the kitchen with a bottle of barbecue sauce in answer to Mark's request for his favorite condiment. That left only Tyler.

Kara's glance rested on him for mere seconds but it was enough to make him aware of her scrutiny. He turned and stared back across the table without hesitation. His dark eyes searched hers, issued a clear challenge. Then, he slowly began to smile with satisfaction. "Yes, Kara?"

Kara felt like her whole body had melted. She was a chocolate bar left on the dash of a car; a waxy crayon liquefied by the summer sun; a wildflower, wilted by a sizzling July without rain. As Tyler's grin spread, so did her sense of befuddlement.

She couldn't speak. Couldn't think. Could hardly

draw an even breath. Dear Lord, what was the matter with her? Why did everything about Tyler Corbett suddenly seem to thrill her? Why did she keep thinking about running her fingers through his thick, dark hair? Why were his eyes so beguiling? What made the sound of his voice so captivating? And that killer smile! *Oh, dear.*

Kara swallowed the lump in her throat. "I—I was just wondering..." *What? Say something! Anything.* She finally managed to stammer, "...how...Road Kill was doing."

"Great. He gets around on three legs as well as Buster does on four. I was kind of surprised you didn't ask about him when you first got here."

She made a pouting face. "I had other things on my mind, thanks to my sneaky sister."

"Yeah, well..." Tyler continued to grin over at her as he rubbed his right cheek with a melodramatic flair. "Whatever you say."

She did a quick flashback to their scene behind the barn and realized he was purposely hassling her. That helped strengthen what little was left of her self-assurance. "If you're going for the sympathy vote, Corbett, I suggest you get your facts straight. I slapped you on the other side."

"Are you sure?"

"Positive."

"Oh. Well, then..." Switching hands, he concentrated on the left side of his face. "Hey. You're right. This is the one that hurts."

"So glad I could help," Kara said, her words mocking.

Susan interrupted. "Okay, you two. Enough already. Let's eat, shall we?" She bowed her head and folded her hands in her lap. "Mark, would you please say grace?"

As Mark began to pray, Kara chanced a peek at Tyler through her lowered lashes.

He was looking back at her the same way.

Kara didn't think the meal would ever end. She'd picked at her food and pushed it around on her plate until it was cold, eating very little. Tyler, on the other hand, seemed famished. She watched him surreptitiously, wondering how anyone could eat when there was such an undercurrent of tension in the room. When Susan got up to clear away the dishes from the main course, she jumped to help her, just as she always had. So did Louise.

"Mark and I can handle this," Susan said with a bright smile. "The rest of you just sit there and relax. I made fruit compotes for dessert." She cocked her head at her husband. "Come on, dear. You can help me carry everything."

As Mark and Susan left the room, Louise settled back down in her chair and urged Kara to do the same. "Let your sister play the hostess," she counseled. "After all, she is entertaining her husband's boss." She cast a motherly look of affection across the table. "Besides, I want you to tell me all about this dog you call Road Kill."

"Tyler rescued him," Kara said. "That's really all there is to tell." She thought back to the rainy night she'd answered the door to the animal hospital and found the handsome Good Samaritan standing there, cradling the injured puppy inside his coat. The vision brought a temporary lump to her throat. She swallowed hard. "It was pretty terrific of him to stop to help a dog that wasn't even his."

"He's always done things like that, even when he was little," Louise said.

That surprised Kara. "You knew him then?"

"Oh, yes. Our families were neighbors. His mother and I were so close he sometimes forgot himself and called me mama, too."

Touched, Kara decided not to comment.

"Tyler used to bring home all kinds of mangled creatures when he was a boy," Louise continued. "I remember one time he found a butterfly with a torn wing in my yard and wanted me to tape the wing to make it better. When I couldn't, he cried all the way home."

"Louise!" Tyler glowered at her.

"Well, you did."

"I don't doubt it," he said. "I just don't think we need to discuss what I was like as a kid."

Kara smiled warmly at Louise and ignored Tyler's outburst. "I think it's sweet. I haven't thought of this in years, but I had a butterfly collection when

I was about seven or eight. It was beautiful. Then, one day, I felt sorry about killing the butterflies. I didn't know that most of them only live a few days, anyway. So I held a private funeral and buried the whole box in the backyard.''

"And now you save animals' lives," the older woman added. "How wonderful."

"I try."

"I understand your husband was also a veterinarian."

Kara cringed internally. Obviously, Tyler hadn't told Louise about his feud with Alex. Silence hung in the room like morning mist over the Spring River. She fidgeted.

Louise reached out and touched her arm. "I'm sorry, dear. I didn't mean to upset you."

"You didn't. I'm fine. Really." She purposely changed the subject. "You should drop by Tyler's to see how cute Roady is before you leave the ranch."

"Oh, good," Louise said, beaming. "I'd love it. We can go together and you can give the puppy your professional attention while I fuss over him."

Kara withdrew. "Oh, I don't think…"

"Nonsense." Louise was patting her hand and smiling triumphantly. "I'm sure you'd like to look in on him. And if we're both there, you won't have to worry about my son-in-law getting out of line again, either."

Eyes wide with surprise, Kara glanced over at Ty-

ler. The look of astonishment on his face was ludi-
crous enough to make her laugh aloud and turn back
to Louise to say, "Thanks. I hadn't thought of it
quite like that."

Tyler grumbled unintelligibly.

Kara could tell he was getting so aggravated he
might bolt. She didn't want Susan's dinner party to
be ruined, so she leaned closer to Louise and spoke
aside, pretending to share a confidence but making
sure her voice was loud enough to be heard across
the table. "It was a surprise when he kissed me, but
it wasn't all that bad, considering." She paused,
then added, "I suppose I shouldn't have slapped
him. It was just a reflex."

Tyler broke in. "Not all that bad? Hey, thanks."

"You're quite welcome." Kara barely managed
to keep a straight face. "I do apologize for clobber-
ing you."

Acting sullen, he rubbed his cheek again. "You
should."

That melodramatic act was all Kara's overloaded
emotions could take, given the fact that she'd been
as edgy as a lone cat at a dog show ever since he'd
arrived. She lost control and burst into laughter.

As soon as she could catch her breath enough to
speak, she said, "How many times do I have to tell
you, Tyler? It was the *other* side I slapped!"

By unanimous consent, everyone had retired to
the patio to enjoy the evening breeze while they

shared pleasant, after-dinner conversation.

Kara noticed that Tyler couldn't seem to sit still.

Finally, he got to his feet and excused himself. "Thanks again for the fine meal, Susan, Mark. I really have to be going. Morning comes early on a ranch, even on Sunday." He swatted at a mosquito that was homing in on his arm. "Besides, I'm about to be eaten alive."

"Me, too," Louise said. "Come on, Kara, dear. Let's walk him home and look in on that puppy of yours."

"Oh, he's not mine." She hung back.

Tyler shook his head and muttered with disdain. "You might as well give in and do what Louise says. Believe me, she's not going to be satisfied until you do. I know. I used to be married to the younger version of her. Dee was a wonderful person but she did inherit a stubborn streak."

That was the first time Kara had heard him say anything about his late wife that was even remotely critical. Usually, he praised her as if she'd been ideal. Perhaps she had been. Deanne Corbett had already been ill the few times Kara had seen her, so there was no telling what the woman had really been like.

Deciding it was prudent to use Louise as a neutral third party, as she'd suggested earlier, Kara looked to her sister. "I'll go check the pup, then come back and help you straighten up."

Susan's, "Fine. Take your time," made Kara grimace. She fell into step beside Louise. More time with Tyler was *not* what she needed. Time *away* from him, however, sounded like a really good idea.

He'd started home without waiting for anyone. Watching his broad back, his athletic walk, Kara wished the night were darker so she couldn't see him; so she wouldn't have to struggle to keep from appreciating the way he looked, the way he moved.

Searching her heart, she sensed that there was more to her current perplexity than merely a superficial temptation. For some unknown reason she cared about Tyler; how he felt, how he thought, what he did. And how he hurt for his loss.

That was the crux of it. It had to be. Because they had both lost mates she was feeling unduly sympathetic toward him. Was he having the same kind of reaction to her? she wondered. Sometimes it seemed that way. At other times, well...Tyler Corbett was an enigma.

Kara huffed in self-derision. Tyler wasn't unique in that respect. *All* men were confusing to her. They always had been. If she'd known how to understand them in the first place, she'd never have been fooled into thinking she was in love and married Alex.

She slowed her pace to match the older woman's and watched Tyler turn the corner by the barn and disappear from their sight.

"I've been wanting to talk to you, alone," Louise said.

They stopped walking. In the moon's light Kara could see lines of worry shadowing the older woman's face. She reached out to her. "Are you okay?"

"I'm fine. It's Tyler I'm concerned about. He's practically been a recluse since my daughter's illness. When I saw him kissing you, it was like a miracle. My prayers were answered."

"Sometimes things are not what they seem," Kara cautioned. She thought about how hard she'd prayed that Alex would ask her to marry him. When he finally did propose, she'd been certain it was because of divine intervention. How wrong she'd been! That thought made her add, "And sometimes it's best if the Lord refuses to give us what we ask for."

Tears glistened in Louise's eyes. "I know. The hardest part for me is always letting go and leaving it up to God to decide what's best for those I love."

Kara took her hand. It was trembling. "I'm so sorry about your daughter."

"She did love Tyler," Louise whispered, "but she wouldn't have wanted him to brood. He needs to find love again. To know that God's looking out for him, guiding him to accept what's been and to look forward to what can be." She squeezed Kara's fingers. "Give him a chance to do that?"

Once again, Kara's conscience reared up to sit atop her heart. "I'd never purposely hurt anyone," she said sincerely. "But I can't promise you anything else."

"That's quite enough, dear. I'm sure God will handle the rest His way, when the time is right. He always does."

Kara knew she should stop rehashing the past and agree completely, yet she kept thinking of all the mistakes she'd made. Had the Lord actually sanctioned her marriage to Alex? Or had He merely permitted it because she'd strayed from the path she should have followed? Probably the latter, she reasoned. If she'd gone against God's will, the problems that resulted were her own fault.

So what about now? What about Tyler? Was she merely dealing logically with a frustrating situation or was she playing with fire? The smartest course would be to call off the whole charade and eliminate the danger of...

Of what? Tyler Corbett posed no threat to anyone, least of all her. He might have a grumpy side but he could also be a funny, entertaining companion. The next prospective suitor Susan dredged up for her might be far harder to deal with. He also might have a different agenda with regard to romance. At least Tyler wasn't actually courting her.

She sighed. She'd wanted a perfect way to deter her sister's matchmaking efforts and that was *exactly* what she'd found. A man who wasn't interested in making a serious commitment was the answer to a prayer. The ideal solution.

So why did she feel so uneasy?

Chapter Seven

Road Kill hobbled to the door, barking, when Kara and Louise stepped onto the ranch house porch.

Kara spoke to him through the screen door. "Hello, boy. Remember me?" She was instantly rewarded when he stopped yapping at her and began wriggling all over with delight.

Louise laughed. "I'd say he remembers you. Look at that! I've never seen a dog wag his tail in a circle."

"He's just full of new tricks," Tyler called from inside. "Let yourselves in. I'm busy picking up the trash that idiot dog scattered all over the kitchen."

"Oh, dear." Louise pulled open the screen door. "I suppose we'd better go help him before he boots our little friend out on his fuzzy ear."

"Or worse." Lifting the pup gently, Kara looked

him over as she followed the older woman through the house. "Except for some mustard on his cast, he seems to be fine. I hope he didn't eat anything bad for him."

Her eyes widened as she entered the kitchen behind Louise. There was shredded paper and assorted household trash spread from one end of the room to the other, beginning at an upended plastic receptacle that lay on its side by the end of the beige, tile-topped counter. Beneath the clutter, the floor was speckled with a delightful array of color. Unfortunately, it looked like the flooring was supposed to be plain off-white, or some similar hue.

Kara held tight to the little brown pup and stifled a giggle. Crouched in the middle of the floor, Tyler was stuffing handfuls of paper into a black plastic trash bag. Seeing that his master had joined the game, Road Kill squirmed and whined to be put down.

"Oh, no, you don't," Kara warned. "It wouldn't be a very good idea to try to play with your daddy right now."

Tyler mumbled a curse. At least Kara thought he did. She decided it was best not to ask for clarification. Instead, she said, "Uh, can I help?"

He looked up at her, scowling. The frown deepened when he saw the mischievous dog in her arms. "Yes. You can take that poor excuse for a pet with you and leave me in peace."

"I meant, can I help you clean up the mess?"

She held the puppy to her and stroked the soft fur on his head. "It's not Roady's fault you didn't have sense enough to put the trash can where he couldn't get to it." She had a further thought. "Besides, how do you know Buster didn't do this?"

"He never has before," Tyler countered. "Why should he start now?"

"Maybe because he has a rival in the house." Kara glanced around the room, assessing the damage. Empty food cans lay in a loosely made group beneath the round dining table; the kind of group a retriever might instinctively make. "Where is Buster, anyway? I didn't see him on the couch when we came in." She leaned down to get a better look under the table. "Aha!"

Tyler pivoted. "Now what?"

"Oh, nothing. I just happened to notice a big yellow dog hiding over there." She pointed. "He looks pretty guilty to me. Of course, he can't be Buster because your wonderful dog would never get into any trouble."

"Well, I'll be." Tyler's jaw dropped. There lay his paragon of canine virtue with an empty dog food can trapped between his paws. Telltale bits of gravy painted a stripe across the top of his nose from where he'd tried to stick his whole muzzle into the can while he licked it clean.

Amused, Kara couldn't resist adding to her earlier comments. "I told you one little dog couldn't have made this big a mess. He's not tall enough to have dumped the trash bin over by himself, either...not to mention having one leg in a cast.'' She ruffled the puppy's pendulous ears and it licked at her hand. ''Daddy didn't mean it, Roady. He's not mad, anymore. Honest, he's not.''

''Daddy?'' Louise said with a giggle. ''Oh, my.'' She crossed to the enclosed back porch. ''I'll go fetch a broom, two if I can find them, and a dustpan. Don't do anything rash while I'm gone.''

Kara was surprised that no physical effort was necessary to coax Buster out from under the table. Tyler merely drawled, ''Buster...'' in an authoritarian voice and the old dog crept over to him, then rolled on his back in submission.

With a sigh, Tyler gave in and scratched the dog's tummy, speaking to him as if he could understand every word. ''You, my old friend, are in serious trouble.'' He pointed to the nearest remaining refuse. ''See this? You know better than to dig in the garbage. What's the matter with you, anyway? You getting senile?'' He glanced up at Kara. ''*Can* dogs get senile?''

''They can lose some of their sharpness,'' she said, smiling down at the touching scene taking place in the middle of the messy floor. ''I don't see that as Buster's problem, though. I think the opposite may be true.''

''Explain.'' Tyler straightened and brushed himself off.

''I think he may be feeling more like a pup, again,

because of having Road Kill around. I'll bet they had a wonderful time ripping all this tasty stuff to shreds. I wish I could have been here to see it."

"You mean to stop it, don't you?"

"Well...no." Kara's grin widened. "I think I'd probably have let them have their fun for a little while, as long as I was sure they couldn't hurt themselves."

"That figures."

She didn't like the snide expression on his face and she said so. "Stop looking at me like that."

"Like what?"

"Like *that*," she said, pointing at him.

Tyler knew he shouldn't encourage her, especially since he'd already been dumb enough to kiss her, but the natural comedy inherent in the situation got the better of him. Instead of remaining his usual aloof and dignified self, he said, "You mean like this?" then scrunched up his face, crossed his eyes, and purposely played the fool.

He heard a strangled gasp. Louise was standing in the doorway, broom in hand, staring at him as if he were demented. Then, she broke into gales of laughter. So did Kara.

Tyler's face reddened. What in the world had made him act like that? He certainly wasn't in the habit of making faces at pretty women. The thought deepened his color. Kara *was* pretty, in a natural sort of way. He just wasn't happy that he'd noticed.

He relieved Louise of the cleaning supplies. "If

you two are through having fun, I suggest we get this mess cleaned up before it sets. I'll sweep and Kara can scoop." Raising an eyebrow he passed Kara the dustpan, fully expecting an argument. He didn't get one.

"Fine." She handed the wriggly puppy to Louise. "If you don't mind, I'd appreciate having his cast washed off so he doesn't start chewing on it. It's not like the old plaster ones. You can get it wet. Just try not to get any water inside, next to his skin."

Louise looked back and forth between the other two, like a spectator at a tennis match, then nodded. "Okay. We'll be in the bathroom if you need anything else. Come on, Buster. You could use a sponging off, too." Head hanging, the old dog followed at her heels.

Once they were alone, Kara faced Tyler and gave him a furtive smile. "Well, I think we did it."

"Did what?"

"Fooled everybody. Didn't you see the way Louise looked at us just now? She's sure we're hiding something."

"We are," Tyler replied. His ingrained defenses sprang into play. "We can't stand each other."

"If you insist."

She'd immediately looked away but he could tell he'd hurt her feelings. Her voice had lost its elation and there was a definite hint of dejection in her posture. Tyler flinched. Like it or not, he cared that he was the cause of her unhappiness.

"I didn't mean it that way," he alibied gruffly. "It just slipped out. Force of habit, I guess."

Kara was about to smile at him and offer forgiveness when he added, "You're not so bad."

She let her sarcastic tone convey far more than her words as she smiled sweetly and said, "Wow. Thanks a bunch, Mr. Corbett. That's the nicest compliment anybody's given me for ages."

"I can't win with you, can I?" His brows knit.

"I didn't know we were having a contest," Kara snapped back. "And stop glaring at me. You look like you'd love to use that broom to sweep me right out the door."

"Don't tempt me."

She faced him squarely, her hands on her hips, and scoffed, "Take your best shot, mister. I was married to Alex Shepherd. After that, *nothing* fazes me."

It was the surprised, shocked look on Tyler's face that made her realize how revealing her statement had been. She hadn't meant to disclose so much, especially not to him. It had slipped out. Denial or explanation, at this point, would only make things worse. The best choice was to try a distraction.

Kara thrust the dustpan at him. "Here. You finish getting the worst of it off the floor and I'll mop up the sticky stuff." When he made no move to follow her orders, she added, "The other option is for me to forget about helping and go on home. I would, except I figure I owe you. So, what'll it be?"

"The mop is in the tall cupboard over there. So's the bucket." He pointed. "Soap is on the shelf above."

She wasted no time. Jerking open the cupboard door she grabbed the mop and bucket, then looked up at the shelf. The soap was there, all right. It was also far too high for her to reach unless she stood on a stool. Having none, she dragged a chair from the dining table and climbed up on it.

Tyler'd had his back turned while he repacked the plastic trash receptacle. He turned in time to see Kara balanced precariously on the chair. "What do you think you're doing?"

"Getting the soap. I'm too short to reach it."

He started across the room. "Why didn't you say so? I'll help you."

"No need. I'm used to coping," she answered, straining to grab the large box of powdered detergent.

At that moment, Tyler reached the chair. In his haste he didn't notice a spot of grease on the slick floor. He slipped. One foot shot out behind him. Momentum slammed him into the backs of Kara's knees.

Her legs buckled. She flailed her arms. The soap powder went up in the air, then rained down on them like winter's first snow.

With a screech, she grabbed the edge of the shelf to stop her fall. Her heart was pounding, her breathing ragged. She was about to confront Tyler and lecture him about safety when the third member of their cleanup crew ran back into the room, accompanied by both dogs.

Louise's mouth dropped open when she saw what was going on. Tyler's arms were outstretched as if he were about to grab Kara around the middle and jerk her off the chair. Kara's eyes were wide with surprise. Louise found her voice enough to squeak, "What in the world are you two doing?"

Kara realized how the situation must look. She giggled. "Would you believe, getting the soap to mop the floor?"

"Not for a minute," the older woman retorted.

Kara had quickly finished mopping the floor, bid Tyler and Louise good-night, and stopped back at Susan's, as promised. The lights were still on so she knocked.

"Come on in," Susan called. She was drying her hands. "You waited just long enough. The dishes are all done and Mark's gone to bed."

"Hey, great." Kara gave her sister a hug. "I always was pretty good at timing my entrance."

"No kidding. Want a midnight snack?"

"It can't be that late!"

Susan chuckled amiably. "Not quite. Is there some rule that it has to actually be twelve o'clock before you can have a *midnight* snack?" Not waiting for a reply, she retrieved what was left of the roast and set the platter on the table.

"I don't think so." Kara got herself a cold soda, plunked down in the chair next to her sister, and picked a sliver of the tender meat to nibble. "This tastes good. Guess I am hungry."

"That makes sense. You didn't eat any dinner."

"I did so."

"Only if pushing it around on your plate counts. But I can understand your problem. It's hard to concentrate on eating and make eyes at Tyler at the same time."

"I did not make eyes at him!" Amazed, Kara stared at Susan. "What makes you think I did?"

"Personal observation," Susan said with a knowing smile. "And it's about time, too. You've been grieving for far too long." She reached to give Kara's hand a reassuring pat. "I know that different people handle loss at different speeds, but it hurts me to see you going on and on alone. I know you can find the same kind of happiness you had with Alex if you'll just open your eyes and look for it."

Kara's throat constricted. She began to cough.

Susan leaned closer and patted her on the back. "Are you okay? Did you choke on your soda?"

"No...I don't know," Kara managed between coughing spasms. Finally she settled down, breathless, and wiped tears from her eyes. Weariness loosened her tongue. She sighed. "I wish you were right about happiness."

"I know I am," Susan insisted. "You'll find

somebody else some day. I pray for you all the time.''

Kara cleared her throat, then made a sound of pure derision. ''Well, don't ask for another man like Alex when you pray, okay? That's the *last* thing I need.''

''What are you talking about?''

''My wonderful husband,'' Kara said flatly. ''He wasn't.''

''Wasn't what? Wonderful?''

''Bingo. Now you're getting the idea.''

''Nobody's perfect.'' Susan reached out to her again. ''All you have to do is look at the rest of us to know that.''

''Yeah, well…'' Suddenly needing Susan's moral support more than ever before, Kara decided to reveal a few extra details. ''Alex was a fraud.''

''What do you mean?'' Susan was frowning.

''He pretended to be kind and considerate when he was in public but he wasn't like that at all when we were alone.''

''He wasn't?'' The frown deepened. ''Is that why you stopped getting together with your old friends or going to church regularly after you got married?''

''That was part of it. I was naive enough to let Alex pick my friends. He also said he didn't want to associate with all the hypocrites in our church and he didn't want me to go, either. But that was just an excuse to change to a church with more people who could enrich his practice. He was the biggest hypocrite of them all.''

Susan sat back, awed. ''I don't believe this.'' She quickly corrected herself. ''I mean…I *do* believe it, I just don't know why you never said anything before.''

''What would have been the use? I married him for better or for worse. We just never got to the *better* part.''

''Oh, honey…'' Susan leaned forward, her unshed tears glistening. ''I'm so sorry.''

''Yeah. So am I,'' Kara said. She managed a smile. ''But that's all over now, so let's forget it. Okay?''

''If that's the way you want it.''

''It is. I just needed you to understand where I'm coming from.''

Instead of the continued somber outlook she'd expected, Kara was surprised to hear her sister say, ''Actually, it's not where you've been or who's hurt you in the past that concerns me. It's where you're *going* that's important.''

There was no way Kara could refute such a basic truth. ''You can understand why I'm in no hurry to remarry, though, can't you?''

''Sure. You don't trust the Lord, anymore.''

Dumbfounded, Kara stared at her. ''I do so.''

''Really? Then why isolate yourself the way you have been? If you were trusting God to take care of you, there'd be no reason to hide from life.''

"I'm not hiding from anything. I'm just being careful."

Susan was slowly shaking her head. "I don't buy that. I think you've decided that it isn't safe to care about another man so you've shut them all out." The corners of her mouth began to lift. "Well, all except one."

Tyler Corbett. Kara opened her mouth to explain, then decided against it. Telling Susan the truth about Alex had obviously been a mistake. The only way to salvage any privacy from the current situation was to continue with the romance charade, at least for a while. Once Susan settled down and quit trying to find her another husband, she'd be able to back away from the pseudo-relationship with Tyler without undue notice.

It was Kara's intention to sound secretive when she said, "I don't want to talk about Tyler." Instead, her words came out in a rush and she noticed she was breathing rapidly.

One look at Susan's smug expression told her she'd been successful in spite of herself. Clearly, Susan was assuming her baby sister was romantically interested in the enigmatic rancher, which was exactly what she'd wanted. The trouble was that interest was no longer a meaningless fabrication! Like it or not, she *was* interested in him.

Sighing inwardly, Kara shook her head slowly and tried to pull herself together as she searched for some positive element in the shocking self-revelation. It finally came to her. She'd hated the idea of lying to anyone for any reason, especially Susan. Now, she wouldn't be lying.

Disgusted with herself, Kara pulled a face. What kind of progress was *that?*

Chapter Eight

Kara had just about succeeded in putting the preceding weekend out of her mind when Louise unexpectedly showed up at her house.

Greeted by three levels of barking and a tan-and-white greyhound who raced around her car in wide circles, she waved to Kara, parked and got out. "Hi! I can see why your sister warned me to wear my jeans when she gave me driving directions. You have quite a menagerie."

"This is only part of it. The horse and most of the cats are back by the barn." She shouted, "Okay, boys. Go on," and the canine welcoming committee obediently fell back.

"Wow. I'm impressed," Louise said. "What's your secret?"

"They think I'm the Alpha dog," Kara explained. "They respect me so they try to do what I want."

"Oh, I get it. You're the leader of the pack!"

"In a manner of speaking. Come on inside and I'll show you my birds. I always clean house first thing Saturday morning, so the place is fairly neat." She refrained from adding that she'd been so uptight all week that she'd dusted and vacuumed every evening rather than sit still and give herself too much time to think.

Louise followed her up onto the covered wooden porch. "This is lovely. So peaceful and quiet." She glanced at the three dogs who had taken up places on the shady lawn and already looked sleepy. "Well, most of the time, anyway."

"It's a lot to take care of," Kara told her, "but I can live here pretty cheaply and the neighbors are far enough away that they don't complain...much." She rested her hand on the head of the tall greyhound at her side without having to bend over. "So, what brings you all the way out here?"

"An errand of mercy," Louise said.

Kara hesitated only a moment, then sighed. "Uh-oh. Sounds serious. I just made a fresh pitcher of lemonade. Would you like some?"

"Yes, please."

The greyhound waited at the open door for the signal to come in as Louise sidled past. Kara smiled down at him and stepped aside. "Okay, Speedy. Come on."

He shot past her and dashed up the hall, only to reappear seconds later, tongue lolling, eyes bright, to leap over the back of the rose-patterned, brocade sofa and circle the carpeted living room at a run.

Louise was clearly amused. "I can see why you call him Speedy. Does he ever slow down?"

"That is slow, for him. He's a retired racing dog. You should see him go when he wants to. I could never catch him if he didn't want to be caught. Unfortunately, he's discovered there are real rabbits to chase around here so I've started letting him sleep inside to keep him out of mischief."

Touching the dog's smooth coat as he trotted past, Louise was amazed. "My, it feels so different. Almost like satin. The hair is so short you can hardly feel it. Doesn't he get cold in the winter?"

"And sunburned in the summer if I'm not careful. That's one more reason for letting him stay inside a lot."

Kara led the way into the kitchen, then turned to face her guest. "Okay. Are you going to stop trying to distract me and tell me why you're here, or am I going to have to drag it out of you?"

"Aren't we having lemonade? I'll get the ice." Louise started opening likely cabinets, quickly found what she was looking for, and set two glasses on the counter beside the refrigerator. "It's the least I can do."

"The least you can do after what?" Kara cast a leery glance at the older woman. "You may as well tell me what you have in mind. Worst-case scenario, I say, no."

"Oh, you won't. It's just that I'm not sure how we're going to handle Tyler."

Aha! Now, she was getting to the ticklish part, Kara thought. No wonder she'd seemed so nervous. She waited until Louise had filled the large tumblers with ice and put them on the table before she said, "Well?"

"I just want you to know, Susan had *nothing* to do with what happened. It was all my fault."

Exasperated, Kara put the pitcher of lemonade down so hard it sloshed. "*What* was?"

"Well, I had this big ham bone left over and I thought I was doing a nice thing. I didn't know I shouldn't give it to Road Kill, and…"

"Is he okay? Did he choke on it?"

Louise quickly laid a reassuring hand on her shoulder. "No, nothing like that. He's fine. Well, almost fine, anyway. He loved chewing on the bone. But then Buster took it away from him."

Kara's patience was nearly gone. "Was there a fight? Did Roady get hurt?"

"Goodness no. He just rolled over on his back and surrendered. Only he'd been holding the bone between his front paws and I guess the flavor was still there, so when he didn't have the bone anymore, he started to chew his cast."

"Uh-oh. What did you do then?"

"I tried washing it off, like you'd told me, but that didn't seem to help, so I called Tyler. Boy, was he steamed."

Rather than dwell on thoughts of anger, Kara busied herself filling the glasses while Louise went on with her story. "First, he tried taping up the frayed parts but the whole thing was such a mess the tape didn't stick. Then he got the brilliant idea that if he put hot sauce on it, Road Kill would leave it alone."

"Oh, no." Kara could picture all sorts of results, none of which were desirable. "Did it work?"

"I suppose it might have if the dog hadn't loved the taste and licked at it so fast." She stifled a giggle. "You should have seen it. One minute, Tyler was positive his plan would work, and the next minute we were both chasing that crazy puppy through the house. We wouldn't have caught him, either, if he hadn't stopped to rub his face on the carpet. What a mess!"

Kara sank into a chair, her fingers pressed to her lips to help stifle her amusement. "Oh, how funny. Poor Roady. I can see it now!"

Relieved, Louise asked, "You mean, the stuff won't make him sick?"

"Hot sauce? No. I'm sure he didn't like it, once he realized how spicy it was, but there shouldn't be any lasting harm." She did, however, have one other concern. "What finally became of the cast on his leg?"

"Last I saw of the dog, Tyler had him tucked under his arm and was headed for the barn, talking to himself."

Thinking of her life with Alex she reacted instinctively and jumped to her feet. "Tyler wouldn't *hurt* Roady, would he? I mean, I never would have left him there if I'd dreamed anything *bad* would happen."

"Tyler? Hurt an animal on purpose? Not in a million years. I know that boy as well as I know myself. There's not a mean bone in his body."

"Oh, thank goodness." Kara sagged against the edge of the table. If the same misfortunes had happened to Alex, she'd have been certain someone or something would get hurt.

"I do think Road Kill may need a new cast, though. I don't know how long it was supposed to stay on, but it's only been a couple of weeks, right?" Looking very apologetic, Louise added, "I'm really sorry I made such a mess of things and upset you so."

"You didn't upset me," Kara assured her. "As long as Roady's all right, there's nothing that can't be fixed. I'll go to the office and get things ready. You bring him to me and we'll either patch up the cast he has or fit a new one."

"Oh, dear." Louise's hands started to flutter like two pale butterflies caught in a whirlwind. "Didn't I mention? I just stopped by on my way to my first day on the job." She beamed. "I'm going to be one of those shopper greeters, like you see all the time at Wally-World."

"You're kidding."

"No. Not a bit. I decided I'd been retired too long

and needed to get out more, so I applied and they hired me! Isn't that wonderful?''

"Peachy," Kara grumbled. Her mind was churning faster than Speedy had run when he was in his prime. "Okay. Use my phone. Call Tyler and tell him to bring the dog to the hospital. I'll get Susan to meet us there.''

"Um...that may pose a problem."

"Why?" Kara was beginning to get a sinking feeling in her stomach, not to mention a doozy of a headache.

"Because I already suggested that," Louise explained. "And he absolutely refused to consider it. Kept saying something about money and honor and...oh, I don't know. It made absolutely no sense to me." She cast a hopeful look at Kara. "I don't suppose you make house calls, do you?''

"Not if I can help it."

"That's what I was afraid of." Louise shrugged. "Oh, well, thanks for the lemonade. I have to be going." She started for the door, then paused. "And don't worry, dear. Tyler's very resourceful. I'm sure he'll find a way to mend the cast and keep Road Kill from chewing off the rest of it."

Kara just stood there. Louise knew very well she couldn't abandon any animal that needed her, even if it meant another trip back to the Corbett ranch and another head-to-head dispute with its owner. There must be another way. By the time she heard Louise's car start and back out the driveway, she was already dialing Susan's number in the hopes she could persuade her to bring the puppy to town instead. No one answered.

Talking to herself, Kara slammed down the receiver. It wasn't Roady's fault he was in trouble. If she didn't give in and go to the ranch to repair the damage Louise's folly had caused, he might lose enough support to rebreak his leg where the bones were starting to knit. She was stuck. Trapped. If only Louise hadn't had to report to work…

Kara's eyes widened. Her lips pressed together into a thin line. Every other time she'd seen Louise Tate, the woman had been dressed impeccably. This morning, however, she'd been wearing blue jeans and a plain blouse. Would she have worn that kind of outfit her first day on a new job? Not likely.

"I've been had," Kara muttered as she began to throw medical supplies into a duffel bag. "If that puppy doesn't really need my help, there are going to be a couple of people who hear exactly what I think about their interference. And that's a fact."

Kara found Tyler alone in the main barn. He still held the puppy in his arms. She burst out, "Oh, thank goodness!" without stopping to consider anything but her own relief.

Scowling, he faced her. Sunlight was streaming through the unshuttered windows and the main door. The brim of his cowboy hat shaded his eyes, making him appear even more gruff than usual. Kara didn't care. She was too elated to give his disposition more than a brief notice.

Tyler raised one dark eyebrow. "I see nothing in this situation to be thankful about, unless you count the fact that you've finally come to collect your useless dog." He tried to pass Road Kill to her.

"Oh, no, you don't." She held up her hands, palms out, to ward him off. "I'm only here because Louise told me the cast needs repair." Peering at it, she leaned a little closer. The dog's whole leg was swathed in so much excess elastic bandage it looked three times its normal size. "What have you done to it?"

"Kept it together with whatever I could find," Tyler said dryly. "I don't dare put him down because the minute I do, he starts ripping it off."

"That figures. He's a smart pup. It only took one experience to teach him he didn't have to put up with bandages if he didn't want to." She smiled proudly. "I knew he was special the first time I saw him."

"I'm so glad you're pleased," Tyler said cynically. "What do you suggest we do about it?"

"We?" Kara's smile widened.

"Yes, we. This is as much your problem as it is mine."

"Oh, I don't know about that. It seems to me that you have possession."

"Only because you forced it on me."

"Well," she drawled, "the way I see it, you can

either ask me nicely to repair the cast, or you can hold on to him like that for another four to six weeks, until his leg heals.'' The astonished expression on Tyler's face made her snicker. "Hey, don't worry. It's a plus. You two will form a much closer emotional bond that way.''

"I don't want to bond with this troublemaker. I want to get rid of him just as soon as he's well. Understand?''

"Oh, sure. No problem. So, what'll it be?''

"What will *what* be?" Tyler knew the kind of response Kara was waiting for but he didn't intend to give in unless she forced the issue.

Her smile never faltered. "Okay. I'll spell it out. Do I go home and forget about helping you, or are you going to ask me for my expert assistance?''

Tyler's jaw muscles clenched. "Okay. I'm asking.''

"No, no, no. Politely. The way you'd treat anybody else, if you wanted them to do you a favor.''

One corner of his mouth twitched, lifted slightly, before he got it back under control. Kara Shepherd was obviously enjoying aggravating him and he couldn't help admiring her spunk. It was an aspect of her personality that seemed to strengthen every time they met, which meant the present situation was unlikely to improve on its own.

He decided to capitulate and get it over with. Tucking Road Kill under one arm, he doffed his hat with a flourish, bowed from the waist, and said with an overly sophisticated air, "My dear madam, would you kindly do me the honor of repairing this flea-bitten excuse for a dog before I toss him out on his ear?" He straightened and put his hat back on, resuming his normal tone of voice. "There. How was that? Polite enough for you?"

Kara laughed gaily. "I guess so. I brought some supplies so we could take care of everything on the spot. Would you like me to work on his leg out here, or shall we go into the house to do it?"

He was about to answer when he noticed a familiar-looking shadow inching across the bare ground in front of the barn door. Louise was trying to sneak up on them to eavesdrop! That gave Tyler an idea. If she hadn't heard all of his prior conversation with Kara, she wouldn't have any idea they were discussing veterinary care instead of something a lot more personal.

Raising one finger to his lips, he whispered, "Shush," and softer, "Louise."

Kara's gaze followed his. Sure enough, they had company. "What now?"

"Watch and learn." He was grinning. Raising his voice and enhancing it with alluring sweetness, he said, "I'd like to do it in the *house,* darlin', if you don't mind."

Blushing, Kara understood the ruse perfectly. Trying not to snicker she made her voice a sultry purr and played along. "No, not at all. I never did like doing it in the barn…even when I was with my husband."

Behind her, Kara heard a sharp intake of breath that ended in a high-pitched squeak. If she hadn't quickly clamped her hand over her mouth she'd have burst into laughter in spite of her temporary embarrassment.

Still in character, Tyler shifted Road Kill to one side, slipped his other arm around Kara's waist, pulled her close, and ushered her out the barn door toward the house. As they passed the place where his nosy, former mother-in-law hid, he leaned down to place a believable kiss on the top of Kara's head.

The kiss was meant as a prank. A farce. It wasn't until after he'd acted that Tyler realized it didn't feel nearly as much like a joke as he'd thought it would.

Kara cleared the kitchen table, laid a plastic sheet over it, and told Tyler to spread a layer of newspaper on top of that. Placing Road Kill in the center, she began to unwrap his leg while Tyler held him still.

Thoughts of Louise's clumsy attempt at matchmaking wouldn't stop running through Kara's head. After the illusion of flirtation she and Tyler had created she felt like a misbehaving teenager. A fresh blush warmed her cheeks. "I hope we didn't shock poor Louise too much."

"I hope we *did*," Tyler countered. "Her curiosity is getting out of hand. Next thing we know, she and

Susan will actually join forces. Then we'll really be in trouble.''

Kara finished unwinding the elastic bandage and laid it aside while she concentrated on the tattered cast. "They do seem to think they have to coerce us into seeing each other.''

"They sure do.'' He wished he could let go of the little brown pup and finish this conversation from a safe distance...like maybe Mars! Going across the room or across town definitely wouldn't be far enough. He couldn't believe he'd been so simpleminded, so preoccupied with fooling Louise, that he'd actually kissed the top of Kara's head. What a mistake. Not only had he liked the feel of her silky hair on his lips, it was the first time he'd noticed the clean, floral scent of her shampoo. Worse, he was still close enough to enjoy its lingering fragrance.

Kara looked up at him, studying his expression. "They only feel they have to push us at each other because we haven't done a good enough job of convincing them otherwise.''

"I suppose you're going to tell me you have another wonderful plan,'' Tyler grumbled. "I didn't think much of the last one.''

"Oh? And I suppose it was my idea for you to manhandle me and waltz me past Louise just now?''

"That was a spur-of-the-moment decision.''

Nodding, Kara agreed. "That's been our problem. We've ad-libbed too often. What we need is a definite script and mutually acceptable rules of conduct.''

"You mean make a *list?*" He was incredulous.

"If need be.'' She turned her attention back to the job at hand and cut away what was left of the cast as she continued to explain. "I think it would be best if we talked it all out and made notes. Then we'll each keep a copy of what we've decided, so we know ahead of time what to do."

"Or what *not* to do."

"Exactly."

Tyler leaned down to look her in the eye. "You're serious, aren't you?"

"Completely. If you have a better idea, I'll be glad to listen to it.''

He snorted in self-derision. "I'd rather just tell everybody off and forget it.''

"Get serious. Susan's too stubborn to take no for an answer. And Louise is overly sensitive because of losing her daughter.'' Kara paused. "Sorry.''

"It's okay.'' His voice was purposely empathetic. Maybe she did have a valid point. If they made an agenda and worked out specific guidelines, there'd be no chance of error…like the unforgettable one he'd made when he'd forgotten himself and kissed her. Twice.

Remembering made him decidedly uneasy. "Let's start with a No-kissing rule.''

"Fine with me.'' She refused to look up at him as she spoke. "We'll probably have to hold hands once in a while, though, or nobody will believe we like each other." Waiting, she expected Tyler to respond with, "We don't like each other." Instead, he remained quiet, stroking the puppy evenly to keep it calm while she resplinted its leg.

Finally, he said, "I suppose you're right. Do you mind going that far? Holding hands, I mean."

Kara was glad he had no clue as to how attractive and appealing she thought he was, especially when he was ministering to the injured puppy. She watched the steady rhythm of Tyler's touch on its short fur and marveled at the gentleness in the man's large, capable hands. Would she mind holding one of those hands? Not hardly. Instead of saying so, however, she alibied. "I'll muddle through if you will."

"Good." He sighed in quiet resignation. "Okay. That's settled. What else?"

"I think we should go out to dinner. Somewhere we can talk without being overheard."

Tyler seemed taken aback. "Dinner?"

"Dinner. Tonight works for me," she said flatly. "I'll pick you up. If we're going to get the most out of this, we'll need to be seen leaving together. I can't think of a better place for that than right here."

"I can. Why don't I come to get you at work someday next week? We can make a big deal about it, then."

"Okay. That'll do." Finished with the puppy, Kara washed her hands, dried them on a paper towel, and smiled. "Tomorrow's Sunday, so we're bound to run into each other anyway."

Beginning to see what she was getting at, he studied her upturned face. "You mean...?"

"Of course." The complaisant smile widened. "I'll meet you in church. Save me a seat and we can impress Louise, too." She lifted the puppy and held him close, ruffling his droopy ears. "In the meantime, I'll take our little friend with me and fit him for an Elizabethan collar so he won't be able to reach his leg to chew on it."

"What about our list?" Tyler was backing away.

"You make one, I'll make one, and then we'll combine them," she said brightly. She eyed the table. "I put all my instruments back in my bag. You can just roll up that plastic and throw it away. Want me to stay and help you clean up?"

"No." He waved her off as if she were a pesky insect. "No, just go. Go. Leave me in peace. *Please.*"

Giggling, she tossed a mock warning back over her shoulder and headed for the door with the puppy. "Watch it, Corbett. If I didn't know better, I'd get the idea you didn't like me."

Chapter Nine

When Kara had finally given up and gone to bed that night, her list of no-nos had begun with, "No kissing." It had ended with, "No hugging." There was nothing else in between.

The more she'd thought about Tyler on a personal level, the worse her dilemma had become. Naturally, she wasn't going to embarrass them both by listing the most obvious things she wouldn't do. He knew what kind of woman she was. And she was certain he was the kind of man who wouldn't press her for unacceptable intimacy. That was one of the main reasons she'd agreed to their mutual deception in the first place. She trusted him. It was that simple.

The rest of her feelings, however, were much more complicated. By dawn Sunday morning she'd developed a sizable tension headache. What she'd wanted to do was pull the covers up over her head and pretend it wasn't time to get ready for church. What she'd done instead was choose the most attractive dress in her closet, put on light makeup, and head for town to keep her promise.

The old stone church sat atop a rise, giving it a heavenly quality when viewed from the base of the hill. Folks parked all the way around it. Kara pulled into her usual spot. She'd often heard it said that the pickup truck was the official vehicle of Arkansas. Church parking lots helped confirm that idea. There were at least as many trucks as there were cars, and a lot of the people who drove cars on Sunday had a truck at home, as well.

Kara gathered her bible and purse and hurried into church before she could change her mind. Pausing in the rear of the sanctuary she scanned the backs of the parishioners who were already seated. It was easy to spot Tyler. Dark-haired and taller than half the men present, he was sitting in almost the same spot he'd occupied the week before.

Kara smoothed her softly draped, sea-foam-green dress, gathered her courage, and was just about to start down the aisle to join him when she felt a tap on her shoulder. As usual, she jumped. As usual, it was her sister.

"Morning, kiddo," Susan said brightly. Her husband, Mark, came up behind her. She gifted him with a loving smile and took his hand. "We swung by your place on our way, to offer you a ride, but you'd already left."

Kara could feel her pulse pounding in her temples. She pressed her fingertips to the sides of her throbbing head and took a deep breath. "Thanks, anyway."

"Hey, are you all right?" Susan leaned closer to study her sibling's expression. "You look kind of spaced out."

"I have a terrible headache."

"I wondered why you wore your hair down, today. Too much weekend?" Susan probed.

Kara could hardly tell her the whole truth. "Too much everything. I've thought so hard lately, my brain hurts."

"I'll bet you have. I noticed your truck parked out at the ranch yesterday."

Kara's head snapped up. She looked quickly from Susan to Mark and back again. "You did?"

"I did. And I'm a little miffed that you didn't stop by my house to say hi while you were out there."

"I didn't think you were home," Kara alibied. In truth, once she'd clashed with Tyler and they'd outwitted Louise, she'd been so befuddled she'd forgotten her sister even lived there. "I did try to phone you earlier. Nobody answered."

"I went to have my hair done in the afternoon." Susan patted the smooth curve of the cut at the nape of her neck. "What was it you wanted?"

"I thought you could bring Roady to the office so I could fix his broken leg."

Instantly concerned, Susan forgot all about her new hairdo. "The same leg? What happened? Where is he now?"

Kara sighed again. "Resting in an inside run at the hospital. It's a long story. I'll fill you in, later."

"Good," Susan said. "Right now, we'd better go grab some seats or we won't find three together."

This was it. The first well-planned step. Suddenly as nervous as if she were about to act the lead role in a Broadway play, Kara managed to smile sweetly. Starting to walk away, she said, "You don't have to worry about me. Someone else is already saving me a place."

"Oh, yeah? Who?"

Susan's question was nearly drowned out by the thudding of Kara's heart. The rapid beat echoed in her ears, drummed in her temples, and ricocheted off her rib cage like a pair of rubber-soled sneakers trapped in a whirling clothes dryer.

By the time she reached the pew where Tyler sat she was getting pretty woozy. That was when she realized she'd been holding her breath!

He stood and stepped into the aisle, politely taking her elbow to guide her. "Are you all right?"

"You're the second person who's asked me that this morning. I'm beginning to get the idea I look bad."

"No, no. You look..." He wanted to say, *abso-*

lutely beautiful, but thought better of it. "Fine. You look just fine."

She cast him a disbelieving glance. "Would you be willing to swear to that?"

"I never swear," he countered with a wry smile. "Especially not in church."

Kara nodded a greeting to the woman on her left as she sat down, then turned back to Tyler with a questioning scowl. "Where's Louise?"

"Visiting her sister. The one in Batesville, I think." He lowered his voice. "Don't look at me like that. How was I supposed to know she was going to take off?"

"Does she do that kind of thing often?"

"Not often enough," he said. "When Deanne got so sick, Louise started acting like my shadow—and she's never stopped. I've been trying to get her to lighten up, for her own sake, but she keeps insisting I need companionship."

In that light, Kara attributed a deeper significance to Louise's absence. "Then it's a good sign." Feeling contrite, she looked up at him. "I apologize."

"For what?"

"For misjudging your motives. When Louise wasn't with you, I jumped to the wrong conclusions."

"Why?"

"Because you're a man." Unwilling to witness the judgment she knew must be in his gaze, she lowered her eyes.

"Oh, I see." And he did see. Clearly, Kara's late husband had left behind a powerful negative influence. How sad, when she was otherwise such an amiable person. He noticed that her trembling hands were clasped atop the bible in her lap. The urge to comfort and reassure her was strong. He reached out.

As his warm, strong hand covered hers, Kara's vision got misty. When he said, "It's okay. I forgive you," she was so touched she felt like weeping.

If she'd looked at Tyler at that moment, she knew she would have burst into tears.

All through the service, Kara was acutely aware of who sat beside her. If anyone had asked her to list even one of the important points of the sermon she'd just heard, she couldn't have done it.

The congregation stood to leave. Tyler pivoted and scanned the crowd behind them before turning to Kara. "Okay. What now?"

"Don't ask me. You're the tall one. I can't see a thing from down here."

He nodded. "Sorry. I forgot you were so little."

Kara stood straight, her chin jutting out proudly. "I'll have you know that both my feet reach the ground just fine, Mr. Corbett. Therefore…"

"Therefore," he said with a chuckle, "your legs must be the perfect length. I've heard that joke before. What I meant was, I can see Susan and Mark headed this way. What have we decided to tell them?''

"Oh, dear." She grasped the problem. "We haven't decided yet, have we?"

"Not as far as I know." Tyler flashed a self-assured grin. "Sitting together this morning was your idea, remember?"

"Don't remind me." Kara pulled a face. "I know, I know. You just did."

Tyler reached out, then paused to see what her reaction would be when he took her hand. He saw her eyes widen like a frightened deer, so he raised their joined hands between them and said quietly, "This was on our okay list. Remember?"

When she nodded, he stepped into the aisle and started making his way to the front of the church, tugging her along behind, while most of the other worshipers went the opposite direction.

She gave only token resistance. "I feel like a salmon swimming upstream. Where are we going?"

"Out the side door. It's that or wait till your sister catches up. Last time I looked, she was gaining on us."

"Well, why didn't you say so sooner? Come on!" Still holding his hand, Kara sprinted ahead and ducked through an archway, two steps in front of him.

Tyler was laughing softly. "I would have if I'd known it would light such a fire under you. I thought for a minute there I was going to have to pick you up and sling you over my shoulder like a sack of grain to get you moving.''

"*That's* going on my no-no list, for sure," Kara shot back. "No tossing me over anybody's shoulder, least of all yours."

"Oh? Why not? I promise not to drop you."

They had reached the outer door. Kara flung it open and shot out into the bright sunlight. She shaded her eyes and squinted up at Tyler. "Because I'm afraid of heights. Besides, I could get a nosebleed from the altitude up there."

"Spoken like a true munchkin," he replied with a chuckle. "Now where to?"

That was the first time Kara had thought that far ahead. If they stayed in the parking lot, Susan was sure to catch up to them before they had a chance to discuss strategy. "I'll make a run for my car."

"Okay. Where are you parked?"

"Over there. By the—" Kara broke off as she peeked around the corner of the church. Mark's truck sat directly in front of hers, blocking her exit. The chances of a simple, quick getaway were slim and none. "Look. I have a problem."

"I see what you mean." He made a snap decision. "Come on. My pickup's parked on the side street. We'll take that."

"To where?"

"Does it matter? All we have to do is give Susan the slip, wait till she's gone home, then come back for your truck."

A marvelous thought popped into Kara's frazzled brain. "I know! We'll go to my office and get Roady. It's a perfect excuse to leave together. That way, when Susan finds out, she won't be mad at me for ditching her!"

Tyler wasn't totally sold on her rationale but he went along with it as a temporary measure. Following her around the side of the building to his truck, he opened the passenger door and helped her in while he mulled over what she'd said.

It might be only his imagination, but it seemed to Tyler that Kara was unduly worried about making other people angry. Yes, she was intrinsically kind and therefore wouldn't want to upset anyone, yet there was more to it than that. She visibly tensed whenever she thought someone was cross with her. When she'd had that reaction to him, he'd assumed it was because of their prior conflicts. Now, he wasn't so sure.

Climbing behind the wheel, he started the engine and pulled away from the curb. "Why would Susan be mad at you?"

Kara opened her mouth to tell him, then realized she had no valid answer. She shook her head, bewildered. "I don't know."

"You'll do anything to avoid conflict, won't you?"

"Any sensible person would."

Tyler didn't argue. He merely said, "Would they?"

* * *

Road Kill was so glad to have company he wriggled all over. When Kara opened the gate to the small dog run he paused only long enough for a brief pat from her, then headed directly for the man he considered to be his master. Kara beamed. "See? He loves you."

Casting her a cynical look, Tyler snorted. "Hah! He sees me as a meal ticket—nothing more." But he began to smile as the puppy awkwardly circled his legs. "What is that plastic thing around his neck? He looks like he got his head caught backward in a funnel."

"That's the Elizabethan collar I told you about. It keeps him from reaching his leg to chew on it."

"Oh." When he bent down, the pup collapsed in a heap at his feet and rolled on its back, tongue lolling and tail still thumping wildly.

Tyler scratched its pale pink-and-beige-spotted tummy as he softly said, "You are a no-good, worthless mutt, you know that? You trashed my kitchen and turned my innocent old dog into a delinquent. What am I going to do with you? Huh?" He examined the repairs to the cast as he went on. "Well, don't just lay there. Speak up. What have you got to say for yourself?"

Road Kill raised his head and looked at the man quizzically. An instant later, he lunged.

Caught off guard, Tyler rocked back on his heels, lost his balance, and wound up sitting on the floor.

That was all the advantage the puppy needed. He jumped into Tyler's lap, cast and all, and planted a wet kiss right in the middle of his cheek!

Kara would have loved to comment but she was laughing so hard she couldn't talk.

Tyler stayed on the floor long enough to gain the upper hand. Gently but firmly, he insisted that Road Kill sit when he was told, even though the puppy quivered with the effort.

"Good boy. That's it," Tyler said. He looked up at Kara. "Maybe you were right. Maybe he is smarter than I gave him credit for."

She was still trying to recover from seeing him sprawled on the cement floor with Roady's cast poking him in the stomach. "Whoa. Do you mean to say *you* were *wrong?*"

"It does happen once every ten years or so," he countered wryly. "But I could be wrong about that, too."

"Then that's twice in one day. By your reckoning, you should be safe from error for the next twenty years."

Muttering, "Don't I wish," Tyler got to his feet and dusted himself off. The puppy immediately began to frolic at his feet again. He looked at it and shook his head. "I suppose you expect me to take him with me."

"It would be best. I only left him here overnight because I was afraid he'd get hurt if my dogs got to roughhousing with him too much. Your house is better because Buster is more laid-back.''

Tyler stuffed his hands into his pockets and watched the pup investigate a corner of the room by hopping on three legs and swinging the longer cast out to the side. ''Buster *used* to be laid-back—and well-behaved—until a certain bad influence polluted his mind.''

''Dogs are scavengers. It's natural for them to rob the trash. Smart owners eliminate the temptation by keeping their refuse out of reach.''

''Are you trying to tell me I made a *third* mistake, Doctor? That's preposterous.''

She watched his countenance darken, his eyes narrow. Then the corners of his mouth began to twitch upward. He was making fun of her! And she'd almost taken his criticism seriously. Talk about mistakes.

Intent on distracting her companion and herself, Kara opened the door to the corridor leading to the outside runs. Raucous barking was the instant result. She had to shout to be heard. ''As long as I'm here, I may as well get my chores done. I usually go home and change after church, but all I have to do is feed and water, so it shouldn't be a problem to do it in a dress.''

Joining her, he closed the door so Road Kill wouldn't follow. ''I'll give you a hand. Show me what to do and we can be finished in half the time.''

That surprised Kara. "I didn't bring you here to put you to work."

"I know. You brought me here to con me into taking that useless mutt home again."

Kara smiled up at him sweetly as she handed him the scoop for the dry dog food and lined up six clean dishes on the counter. "Did it work?"

"For the present," Tyler said with a sigh. He waved the empty scoop in the direction of the dishes. "What do you want me to put in these, and how much?"

"One full scoop of kibble and half a can of the gravy-covered stuff in those cases over there." She reached under the table, added one more dish to the group, then said, "Except for this one. It gets three scoops and two whole cans."

Tyler eyed the dish. "That looks like a turkey roaster. Even Buster doesn't eat that much." Pausing, he glanced down the row of dog runs. "What in the world *does?*"

"Big Bertha," Kara said, pointing. "You'll find her in the end run. Go have a look if you want. She's enormous but she's also the sweetest one of the bunch." As he started down the passageway, Kara added, "She drools when she's about to be fed, though. I wouldn't stand too close to the fence if I were you."

Overcome by curiosity, he had to see for himself. The dog he found in the last run looked like a cross between a Saint Bernard and a black Labrador retriever. There was benevolence in her sad, brown eyes and a lethargy to her movements that was somehow restful. She got to her feet and met him at the chain-link gate. Her nose was jet-black, her muzzle droopy, and her tongue wider than Road Kill's whole head. All four legs and her tail were sopping wet, as if she'd been swimming.

Amazed, Tyler called back to Kara. "I see it, but I still don't know what it is."

"I'm not surprised. Bertha's a full-grown New-foundland. They're fairly rare, especially in the south, partly because they suffer so much in the summer heat."

"Is that why you've got a plastic wading pool in there with her? Or does she need that much water to drink?"

Laughing, Kara brought the Newfoundland's din-ner and handed the heavy dish to Tyler to hold while she unlocked the gate to the run. "They like to lie in the water to cool off so I got her a pool of her own. She's actually an easy keeper, considering her size. Newfs are a pretty quiet breed, so they don't expend a lot of energy, especially when they get as old as Bertha."

"What is she, fifteen or sixteen?"

"Oh, no. She's barely seven," Kara said sadly. "The giant breeds have a notoriously short life span." Opening the gate slightly, she ordered, "Sit," then, "Stay" and the dog did exactly as it was told while Tyler placed the food inside the fence.

The dog's gentle disposition and kind expression touched him deeply. What a shame it had grown old before its time. Buster was already fifteen and he was just beginning to show his age. Tyler straightened and backed away while Kara latched the gate.

"I have to lock this one because Bertha's so smart," Kara explained. "She taught herself to unfasten the simple catches that I use to keep all the other dogs in."

"It must be sad to love a magnificent animal like that, only to lose it so young."

"I suppose you could look at it that way. I think the people who choose to own one of the giants feel that a little time with a dog like this is worth whatever heartache comes afterward. Most of them get another dog just like the one they lost, in spite of knowing the same thing will probably happen again." Kara suddenly realized the bittersweet turn their innocent conversation had taken. Holding her breath, she hoped and prayed that Tyler would not make the same connection.

"It's because they're looking for the same perfect love they found before," he said pensively. "I wish the rest of life was that easy."

What could she say? That he'd find another wife as wonderful as the one he'd lost? Platitudes were not only useless, they would cause him more pain. According to everyone who knew Tyler, he'd elevated his late wife to the level of a saint. It didn't matter that no normal mortal could ever be that perfect. As long as he thought Deanne had been a saint, he'd be content to cherish her memory. Kara was not about to argue with a dream like that.

All she could think of to say was, "I'm so sorry."

When he responded with, "So am I," Kara wanted to wrap her arms around him, hold him tight, and rock away his sorrow the way a loving mother comforts an injured child.

Big Bertha chose that moment to shake, flinging swimming pool water all over everything and shattering the poignant mood.

Tyler shouted and fled. Kara was right behind him. Neither stopped until they were safely back at the other end of the aisle. He was muttering to himself.

"I *told* you to be careful," Kara prompted.

"You didn't tell me she was going to be all wet to start with." He was brushing at his slacks.

"A little water won't kill you." It was Tyler's quiet reaction, the solemn look in his eyes, that made her realize exactly what she'd said.

The temptation to curse was strong. Instead, she waved her hands in the air and closed her eyes. "I'm sorry. I did it again, didn't I? I don't mean to. It's just that our language is filled with expressions like that and I wasn't thinking. I…"

Shaking his head, Tyler stepped closer and stilled her hands by taking them in his and drawing them to his chest. "It's not you. The problem is mine." His fingers caressed hers while he searched for the right words. "Sometimes I let myself dwell on the things that have gone wrong and forget to thank God for my blessings. Like you."

Kara was speechless. Did he mean that she, also, forgot to give God the glory? Or was he saying he considered her one of his blessings? Before she could ask, he answered the unspoken question.

"When I'm with you, I feel…I don't know…kind of liberated. Like it's okay for me to be sad when we're together, because you'll understand and not try to talk me out of it. And it's okay to laugh, too, because you aren't judging me for being too happy when I should still be mourning." He paused, looking into her eyes and searching for the empathy he knew he'd find there. "Does that make sense to you?"

"Perfect sense," Kara whispered. She rested her forehead against their joined hands and closed her eyes. "I feel exactly the same way."

Chapter Ten

It took Kara only a few moments to realize how unacceptably intimate she and Tyler were behaving. It took a little longer, however, for her to convince herself to break the comforting contact.

She finally stepped back. He let her slide her hands out of his grasp without argument. She knew she should offer some kind of excuse for her behavior. The trouble was she couldn't seem to come up with any reasonable rationalization.

Nevertheless, she made an attempt to explain. "I...we...I mean..."

Tyler's expression was cynical. He nodded. "Yeah. Me, too."

They parted awkwardly. Kara immediately busied herself filling all the outside water dishes with a hose, then went inside to take care of the animals recuperating in smaller cages. She didn't want to even look at Tyler again, let alone engage in any more in-depth conversation with him. What had happened already was bad enough.

He followed her inside. "Where's Road Kill?"

"I saw him headed for the office." Her words were clipped, her tone contentious.

"Oh." Tyler casually strolled closer. "Is there anything else I can do to help?" When she kept on rinsing feeding bowls in the utility sink, pointedly ignoring him, he tried a more direct approach. "Hey, don't be mad at *me*. Holding hands was on the 'okay' list, wasn't it?"

It was his virtuous attitude that irritated her the most. To listen to him, a person would think they hadn't just looked through a mutual window into both their souls. Anger was her best—her only—defense against that kind of unwelcome closeness.

She sent a brief, icy stare his way. "I meant in public. When we want to be convincing."

"Oh. Sorry." Tyler stuffed his hands into his pockets as if hiding them would negate the social error. He stood back and watched her for long moments. "Speaking of lists, I had some trouble making mine. How about you? Did you come up with many rules?"

"No." She tossed her head to sweep her long hair back over her shoulders without touching it while she dried her hands on a clean, white towel. "I had a terrible time deciding."

"So how many did you write down?"

Kara made a face. "Two. But I've since thought of a couple more. Like, 'let's not be nice to each other when we don't have to be.'"

"You don't mean that."

"Oh, yes, I do," she insisted. "Look at us, Tyler. All we have in common is our grief. What kind of basis is that for anything?"

He sensed the enormous protective wall she'd built around her broken heart. How sad to have nothing more than that to represent her years of marriage. And how truly blessed he was to have had the opposite kind of life with Deanne.

Rather than express thoughts that would only intensify Kara's hurt and resentment, he kept silent and gave in. "Okay. If that's the way you want it, that's how we'll do it. But I won't guarantee I'll remember I'm supposed to act unfriendly when we're alone. It's not my nature."

"I know." Kara's voice was barely audible. Then she raised her chin proudly and stood ramrod straight. "Leave the hostile stuff to me. I'm very used to handling it." She saw a new tenderness start to shine through his eyes; a sentiment she wanted no part of. "And stop looking at me like that."

"Seems to me we went over this subject once before, back in my kitchen. So how do you want me to look at you?"

"Not at *all* would be fine with me," she snapped. "I felt like an animal in the zoo when we were in church this morning. Everybody was staring at us and whispering.''

"Well, not everybody," Tyler said with a half smile. "There was that old bald guy in the back pew, second from the left. But I think he was asleep.''

He ducked just in time to miss being hit in the head by the wadded-up towel she chucked at him. Grinning, he caught it as it tumbled past and hefted it in his hand as if testing its weight.

Kara noticed his eyes narrowing while his sly smile spread. She warned, "Whatever you're thinking, Tyler Corbett, don't you dare do it.''

One eyebrow arched. "I didn't start this.''

"Yes, you did. I was trying to be serious and you made fun of me.''

"Of *us,* Kara. Not of you. I know exactly what you mean about feeling like you're always on display. People mean well, but their morbid curiosity gets in the way.''

"Well, maybe." Noting that he was still holding the balled-up towel in his hand, she edged to her left until her hip bumped against the rim of the sink. She'd been rinsing the kennel dishes with warm water from the spray nozzle and the main water supply was still turned on. If Tyler did what she thought he was planning to do, she'd be ready to retaliate immediately.

Looking at her askance, he drawled, "Kara...I

see a funny look in your eyes. What are you thinking?''

''Why, nothing, Tyler.'' The words were coated with far too much cloying sweetness to be believable.

He fisted the towel. ''Get away from the sink.''

''Uh-uh. Not till you put that down and back off.''

''This could get nasty,'' he cautioned.

''I'll take my chances.''

He charged.

She lunged for the sprayer. Grasping it, she swung it toward him without taking aim. As close as he was, she couldn't miss.

Tyler bellowed but kept coming. He grasped her wrist to divert the spray. It shot straight up in the air and rained down on them both like a private cloudburst.

''Let go of me!'' she screeched.

''Not till you turn off the water!''

''I can't,'' Kara shouted. ''You're holding my hand shut.''

''Why didn't you say so?'' Releasing her, Tyler started to laugh. ''You're a mess, Doc. So's your hospital.''

''Well, so are you.'' She was sorely tempted to shoot one last spritz at him. If he hadn't been drenched already, she might have given in to the whim.

''I'm not as bad off as you are,'' he countered,

wiping his face with his hands. "I hope your dress isn't ruined."

"It's washable." Kara looked down at the limp, soggy fabric. "I don't remember if the directions say I'm supposed to take it off first, but I suppose I am."

"Undoubtedly. They probably figured it wasn't necessary to explain that part." Still chuckling softly, he eyed the disorder they'd created. Water dripped from the overhead beams and puddles had formed on the concrete floor, especially where they'd stood. "I think it's my turn to mop," he said.

"It's only water. It'll dry." She handed him a fresh towel. "Here. Your hair's all wet. Just toss the towel into the hamper under the sink when you've finished with it. I have a laundry service."

"Maybe you should jump in the hamper yourself," he quipped.

"Naw. I'll dry, too. Eventually." She glanced at her reflection in the window over the sink. One side of her hair still looked fairly good. The other hung limp and soggy. "I do think it might be best if I didn't go back to get my truck until later, though. No telling what rumors will get started if folks see me like this."

"People mean well," Tyler offered. "They don't know they're doing anything wrong when they pay so much attention to us. I think we scare them."

That gave her pause. "Scare them? How? Why?"

"Because they can identify with us on a basic level. Whether they admit it or not, they know that what happened to us could just as easily happen to them.''

Kara sighed. ''I'd never thought of it quite that way. You may be right.'' A slight smile lifted the corners of her mouth. ''Of course, if you tell anybody I agreed with you about anything, I'll deny it.''

''You mean you'd lie? Tsk-tsk-tsk. Weren't you listening to the sermon this morning?''

''Since you insist on the absolute truth,'' she said stubbornly, ''the answer is, no. I didn't hear a word of it.''

''Why not?''

Kara shook her head slowly as she studied the handsome rancher. His dark hair was tousled from towel drying, his eyes sparkled with wit, his smile made her toes curl every time he flashed it, and his openness made her feel totally unequipped to cope on an equal level.

Starting for the door leading to the rest of the animal hospital, she looked back over her shoulder. ''Only one embarrassing question per customer. You've already used yours. Sorry.''

''Where are you going?''

''To look for Roady and see what kind of trouble he's gotten himself into this time.''

Pensive, Tyler watched her leave the room. *Trouble? Hah!* That scrawny brown pup's antics were nothing compared to what was happening between him and Kara. He was starting to like her. Really like her. They could become friends, perhaps even confidants, if she ever got over being so blasted standoffish.

He sighed deeply. It was easy to believe Kara's claim that she was an expert at handling hostility. She should be, given her past. But there was more to her than that. Much more. Tyler just wasn't convinced that he wanted to get close enough to her to find out what else there was to know.

Kara's dress was still speckled with damp spots by the time Tyler drove her back to the church to get her truck. Road Kill napped on the seat between them, providing the barrier both of them wanted.

When she opened the door to get out, the puppy acted like he expected to go with her. Kara put out her hand to stop him from trying to jump down and hurting himself. "No, Roady. You go home with Daddy."

"I wish you wouldn't keep calling me that." Tyler pulled the pup to him so she could safely close the truck door. "It's embarrassing."

"Don't be silly. There's nobody else here to hear me say it," she countered, waving her arm in a wide arc.

Road Kill cuddled up to Tyler as Kara peered in the half-open window. "Besides, I do see a family resemblance. For instance, you both have brown eyes."

"Sweet of you to notice," Tyler grumbled. "So,

how much longer am I going to have to baby-sit this monster?''

"I'll probably need to work on his leg a couple more times, depending on how fast he's growing. On an adult dog, we could just cast the break and leave it alone, but on a growing pup the dressings can get too tight if we're not careful." She noticed that Tyler had laid his arm across the puppy's back, like an armrest, and was absentmindedly scratching his fur under the Elizabethan collar. Road Kill's eyes glazed over, then drifted half-shut with utter bliss.

Tyler nodded. "Okay. How about this funnel-shaped thing you put on him? When can I take it off?"

"Whenever you want. I'd probably give him a few days, then remove it and watch to see what he does. If he leaves his leg alone, it should be safe to stop using the collar."

"Do you think he will?" Tyler asked.

Kara chuckled. "Not in a million years. He has your stubborn streak, too. Must run in the family."

Susan was lying in wait for her when Kara got home. "Aha! I knew you'd show up here, eventually. You might abandon your only sister and run off after church without a word, but you'd never leave your helpless animals to fend for themselves."

"Did I forget to put out bowls of kibble and water for you, sis? Sorry."

Susan giggled. "You should be." She trailed Kara into the house, continuing to badger her. "Well? Give? What happened with you and Tyler? Where have you been all this time? Do you know it's after three o'clock? I've been going nuts, waiting and wondering."

It suddenly occurred to Kara that she wouldn't have to tell a single fib. Not one! Susan's wild imagination would supply enough lurid details all by itself. "There's absolutely nothing between me and Tyler Corbett," Kara declared, relieved.

"Oh, sure. I saw the way you two looked at each other in church. And then when he hustled you out the side door the way he did, I thought I'd faint. What a hunk!"

"I'm afraid I don't know what you're talking about. We just left that way to avoid the crowd at the other door. There was nothing romantic about it." She almost laughed at the disbelief in her sister's expression.

"Sure, sure."

"It's the truth. Actually, I'd expected to sit by Louise this morning, but she's out of town. I understand she went to visit her sister."

"Oh, yeah, I see. Be nice to the former mother-in-law. Good plan, kiddo. If Louise Tate is on your side, you've won half the battle."

"I'm not being pleasant to Louise because she was Deanne's mother. I happen to like the woman. I probably would have liked Dee, too, if I'd had a chance to get to know her." Pausing, Kara decided to go on. She stared directly at her sister to reinforce the point she was making. "The only thing I *don't* like about Louise is her nosy attitude."

"Oh, really?"

Kara couldn't believe Susan's blameless demeanor. "Yes. Really. There seems to be a lot of that kind of interference going on around here. Have you noticed?"

"Nope." Susan giggled again. "Must be your imagination."

"I doubt it. And if you don't want me to disown you, you'd better not set up any more surprise dinner parties with me as the patsy. Got that?"

"Sure. You don't need my help. At least not anymore. I can't believe how fast you and Ty took to each other. Has he forgiven Alex, too?"

Sobering, Kara shook her head. "I don't know. I haven't asked. Don't you bring it up to him, either. The less said about Alex, the better."

"Was it really so bad…living with him, I mean?" Susan laid a comforting hand on Kara's arm.

Now that Kara had spent a little time with Tyler Corbett, she could see how much she'd missed—would continue to miss—in life, simply because she'd chosen to wed the wrong man. That knowledge intensified the depth of her remorse. "It was what it was," she said softly. "I have no one to blame but myself."

"Why? Because Alex was a skunk? That wasn't your fault, it was his."

"I married him," Kara said flatly. She pressed her lips into a thin line. "I made the choice. That makes it my fault for the way my life turned out."

Susan raised her voice, nearly shouting, "Phooey! You're as bad as Tyler."

"What do you mean?"

Shaking her head, Susan huffed in disgust. "As close as you two have been, lately, I thought you'd know already. He blames himself for Deanne's death. Talk about dumb."

"What?" Kara's knees felt suddenly rubbery. "Why?"

"I don't know all the details. Just what Mark's told me. I guess there was a problem getting the treatment Dee needed, because of the cost involved. Ty finally worked it out by mortgaging everything, but in the meantime, her condition got a lot worse. More than one doctor told him the short delay didn't affect the inevitable outcome, only he refused to believe it."

"Oh, how awful for him." Unshed tears filled Kara's eyes, threatened to spill over. She blinked rapidly to hold them back.

Susan was nodding with comprehension. "The poor guy went through hell. So tell me again how you don't care a thing about him."

What could Kara say? Of course she cared. But that didn't automatically mean there was anything else brewing between her and Tyler. On the contrary. Susan's story further underscored his phenomenal love for his wife. A perfect devotion like that was a once-in-a-lifetime gift from God, not something that could ever be replaced.

Sniffling, Kara turned away to hide the consequences of her overwrought state. Naturally, Susan wouldn't be fooled, it just helped to avoid seeing the sympathy mirrored in her eyes.

"I do care about Tyler," Kara said. "Not for personal reasons, but because I understand what he's going through."

"Is that why you're crying?" Susan asked tenderly.

Within the jumble of Kara's emotions, one unwelcome fact continued to surface until she could no longer deny its existence. All her tears were not for Tyler. Or for his loss. Some were for herself. She'd wasted her chance for the kind of happiness he'd found, and, like it or not, she was envious of a woman she'd hardly known, simply because he'd once loved her.

Oh, Father, forgive me, Kara prayed silently. *I don't mean to be covetous. I just wish…*

Breaking off, she tossed her head stubbornly and started for the kitchen. "Forget it. I'm acting silly. I'll be fine as soon as I can find a tissue and blow my nose." She managed a smile as she glanced back at Susan. "I've been shutting Speedy in the laundry room while I'm gone. Let him out for me, will you?''

"Sure. Why's he in the doghouse?'' Susan was still a bit subdued.

"Because he's tried twice to chase a rabbit by jumping through the screen on the front window. I don't want him to try it sometime when the glass is closed. He'd probably be cut to ribbons.''

"Ugh! No kidding.'' She finally started to smile. "You and your menagerie. I swear, I don't know why you keep taking in so many strays.''

"They don't have anybody else. They need me,'' Kara said. To herself, she added, And I need them for the same reason.

Chapter Eleven

Kara was surprised when Tyler showed up at the animal hospital just after closing the following Wednesday.

Susan unlocked the door to let him in, gave Kara a broad wink, and promptly headed for the kennel area. "Well, there's work to be done. You two take all the time you need. I'll clean up and feed by myself tonight." She giggled as she looked back at her sister. "And, no, I did not invite him to stop by, so you can't blame me this time."

Puzzled, Kara frowned up at Tyler. "What are you doing here?"

He politely removed his cowboy hat and held it casually in one hand. "You forgot we had a date? Shame on you."

"We didn't have a date."

"Yes, we did. You wanted to get together and go over our lists. Remember?"

"Well, yes, but we both said we weren't able to think of much to add, so I figured—"

"You figured I wasn't serious in the first place," he concluded. "I thought you knew me better than that."

"I don't know you at all."

"That's not what you said right before we had the water fight last Sunday."

Kara waved her hands wildly at him. "Hush! Susan will hear you."

"So? We didn't do anything wrong. Unless your dress was ruined after all. Was it?"

"No. At least I don't think so. I just tossed it in the washer and dryer. It looked okay when I took it out and hung it up."

"Good. I like it on you."

"What's that supposed to mean?"

"It means I like the dress. Nothing more. Nothing less," he said, starting to get annoyed. "Now, are we having dinner together, or shall I take the hint and just go away?"

"I didn't mean..." Kara felt about two inches tall. "I'm sorry. It's been a rough day."

"I can see that from here." Looking her up and down, Tyler stopped at her stained white coat and pants. He raised one eyebrow. "I hope the other guy fared better than you did."

"The other guy's fine, thanks." She realized how

she must look. "But I can't go anywhere looking like this. And I didn't bring a change of clothes. Maybe another time."

"Nope. You're not going to brush me off that easy. If I can have my hair cut and take the time to shave—twice in the same day—you're going to go out to dinner with me. Tonight."

She couldn't tell if he was teasing or serious. His hair did look marvelous—dark, shiny and neatly trimmed. As for his lack of beard stubble, all she could see was the compelling cut of his jaw and the way the fine lines on his face accentuated his smile and made his eyes twinkle. "You're pretty sure of yourself, aren't you?"

"I'll be even better once I've seen your list and made sure you haven't added anything scandalous."

Kara gasped. "Me? Don't you dare—" Her sentence was cut off abruptly when he picked her up, swung her feet off the floor, and started to carry her toward the door. "Put me down!"

"Susan!" Tyler shouted over the uproar. "Hey, Susan. Come unlock this door and let me out before your sister gives me a black eye."

"That's a good idea," Kara sputtered. Instead, she pushed against his chest, hoping to break free. It didn't help a bit.

Tyler was laughing. "My second good idea of the day. The first one was when I decided to treat you to a nice dinner. I just didn't dream it would be so hard to get you to go with me." He looked beyond

Kara. "Ah, Susan, there you are. I seem to have a problem. The door's locked and I need to abscond with my date. As you can see, she's being difficult tonight."

"She's *always* difficult," Susan said with a wide grin. Hesitating, key poised, she looked at Kara and added, "I suppose I should ask you if you want me to let him out or call the police instead."

"Look at me! I am *not* going out in public looking like I've just been dragged through the mud," Kara shouted. "I tried to tell him that, but he's not listening."

"Well, why didn't you say so? Wait right there."

In a few seconds, Susan was back with a pile of neatly folded clothes. "Here we go. My favorite denim blouse and jeans to match." She ignored the face Kara was making and spoke directly to Tyler. "Put her down so she can go take a shower and change. I'll make sure she doesn't duck out the back door."

"Well…I don't know. She's pretty sneaky."

"You're telling me. That was quite a disappearing act you two pulled after church last Sunday."

"It *was* good, wasn't it?" He lowered Kara's feet to the floor and carefully released her as he said to Susan, "Let's you and me sit down and have a little talk while Kara's changing. I'll bet you can tell me all kinds of interesting things about her. For instance, was she this stubborn when she was a little girl?"

Kara's loud, "Aargh!" filled the room. She snatched the clean clothes out of Susan's hands and headed for the bathroom next to her private office. The last thing she heard her sister say, was, "You wouldn't believe it. I remember one time, when she was about six and I was ten..."

Picking up her pace, Kara ran down the hallway and flew into the bathroom, shedding her lab coat as she went. The sooner she got back to Tyler, the less time Susan would have to regale him with inventive tales of her childhood.

She jumped into the shower, washing automatically while her memory zipped from one event to another. What had she done when she was only a six-year-old? The butterfly collection? No, that came later. Maybe Susan was referring to the time she'd been caught sneaking food to a dozen stray cats behind her uncle's garage. Nope. Couldn't be that, either. She'd been at least eight, then.

Maybe it was— Oh, no! Not that! Susan wouldn't... Kara gritted her teeth. Yes, Susan would. Especially if she thought it would soften Tyler's heart.

Jumping out of the shower she grabbed a towel, quickly dried herself, and dove into the borrowed clothes. There was no time to waste.

Tyler was lounging in the office chair behind the counter, his boots propped up, when Kara returned. Susan had perched on the edge of the computer desk. They both looked terribly pleased with themselves.

"Okay, break it up," Kara ordered. "I'm ready to go."

"I knew she'd hurry," Susan said aside. "She didn't dare leave us alone too long."

"I have nothing to hide," Kara said flatly. "And I also have all night to get even by telling my version of our family secrets." The pseudoscandalized look on Susan's face led her to qualify her statement. "I didn't mean literally *all* night, and you know it, so don't look at me like that."

Tyler chuckled. "She's been warning me to stop looking at her funny for weeks, and I still don't know what she's talking about."

"Maybe her conscience is bothering her," Susan offered. "She always did have an extra strong dose of scruples. Wouldn't let me get away with a thing. I remember one time, when I was about fourteen—"

"Stop!" Kara ordered. She tugged on Tyler's arm. "Come on. We're leaving."

He feigned reluctance. "Aw, do we have to go? I was just getting interested."

"I'll bet you were." She unlocked the front door, pushed it open before he could do it for her, and pointed stiffly. "Out. Now. Go."

Tyler went without comment. After the fact, Kara realized she'd sounded like an irate parent lecturing a naughty child! That was very wrong. She ought to know. If she'd so much as raised her voice to Alex she'd have been in for a vicious tongue-lashing. The recollection made her stomach churn, her temples begin to throb.

Tyler put his hat back on and sauntered around to the passenger side of his truck. Kara hesitated, waiting for him to turn so she could see his expression and decide if she'd inadvertently made him angry.

He opened the truck door. "Well?"

"Sorry. I'm coming."

Puzzled, Tyler noticed how reluctant she seemed. How she averted her gaze. When she was close enough, he reached out and gently touched her shoulder. Startled, she flinched.

"I didn't mean to scare you," he said quietly.

"You didn't."

"Then what is it? What's wrong?"

His tone was kindhearted. It matched the look on his face, putting her more at ease. She sighed. "Nothing. Nothing's wrong. I just thought…"

"What?"

"It doesn't matter. I was mistaken." She angled past him, climbed into the fancy vehicle, and promptly changed the subject. "This is a really nice truck. Is it new?"

"Compared to the others on the ranch, yes." He got behind the wheel. "I'd wanted one for years but I couldn't convince myself it was okay to buy it. About six months ago, I finally gave in."

"Oh." She couldn't believe how tongue-tied she suddenly felt, alone in the truck with him as they drove away. They'd been together like that before, so what was making her so apprehensive this time?

"Aren't you going to ask me why I waited?"

Kara blinked to clear her head. "Okay. Why did you wait?" Turning to look at him, she noticed his powerful hands clamped hard on the steering wheel and imagined the muscles of his arms tightening beneath the long sleeves of his Western shirt. Quickly, she added, "You don't have to tell me if you don't want to."

Tyler shook his head. "I do want to. I think it may help you if we talk about it."

"Help me? I don't understand."

"You will. I hope." He continued to watch the road. They'd left Hardy and were headed toward Ash Flat. "At first, I didn't know why I wasn't willing to buy the truck. I found lots of excuses to put it off. Then, one day, I realized what was holding me back." Tyler paused to give his declaration more emphasis. "I didn't think I deserved it."

"Why not?"

"Because Deanne wasn't going to be here to enjoy it with me."

A heaviness bore down on Kara's chest. She wanted to reassure him, to tell him he had no reason to continue to feel obligated, yet she couldn't force the words out. When Tyler pulled to the side of the road, stopped the truck and reached for her hand, she didn't resist.

"Do you see what I'm trying to tell you, Kara?

It was a real awakening for me. I had to accept the fact that my life is not over, in spite of my thinking for a long time that it was…that it should be. If I make myself go on, regardless of how I feel at the moment, things will get better. Easier. I'll never forget Dee. I don't want to. But if I deny my individuality, if I withdraw from life, I'm wasting the time and talents the Lord has given me."

"That's pretty profound," Kara whispered.

"I know. I just thought you needed to hear it."

What had it cost him to expose his private emotions like that? she wondered. It couldn't have been an easy thing to do, yet he'd done it. For her. Because he had a kind heart. Her fingers threaded between his and tightened. "Thank you."

Tyler's resulting smile was both benevolent and triumphant. He lifted her hand to his lips and brushed a light, friendly kiss across the backs of her knuckles before letting go. "You're quite welcome, Doc. It was my pleasure. Now, where would you like to go for dinner?"

Kara didn't want to travel far in the intimate confines of the truck so she suggested a small restaurant close by. "How about Bea's?"

"Over on Highway 62? I thought you wanted some privacy so we could talk?"

She wasn't about to tell him she'd had enough time alone with him to last her the rest of her life. Maybe longer. "It's so noisy at Bea's nobody will be able to overhear a thing we say," she countered.

"Besides, tonight their special is catfish. And hush-puppies to *die* for." A few seconds later, Kara squeezed her eyes shut and said, "Oh, no! I did it again."

Tyler was amused. "Hey, don't sweat it. I might not agree to give up my life for a hushpuppy but if that's what makes you happy, fine."

"You know what I meant." She pulled a face. "Every time we talk I seem to put my foot in my mouth."

"Well, spit it out," he said with a laugh. "It'll spoil your dinner."

Bea's Family Café was famous for its country cooking. A restaurant of one kind or another had occupied the same space for over a generation, which was why Kara could still see the faded remnants of other names painted on the side of the building beneath the current sign. As usual, the parking lot contained as many pickup trucks as it did passenger cars.

Seven people greeted Kara and Tyler with a nod, an amiable wave, or a brief Hello when they entered the cramped dining room. The waitress did, too. "Hi, there, folks. Have a seat if you can find one. I'll be right with you."

Kara led the way to an available table in the farthest corner. She'd expected Tyler to sit down across from her. Instead, he took the chair next to hers, trapping her between the wall and his broad shoulders.

She nudged him with her elbow. "Aren't you crowded?"

"Nope. You?"

"Yes, now that you mention it. How about moving over there?" She pointed to the chair she'd wanted him to choose in the first place.

"Too far," he whispered. "We can't talk about personal stuff if I'm way over there." He scooted his padded, metal-framed chair six inches to the left. "How's that?"

"Oh, *much* better," Kara gibed. "I can actually move one arm, now. That should make eating a lot easier."

"I aim to please." He flashed a smile at the approaching waitress. "I don't think we need menus. Kara's been raving about eating your catfish special all the way over here, so we'll have that. And iced tea, please." He looked back at his companion, surprised to see a return of the stress he thought he'd banished. "Did you change your mind about what you wanted?"

Kara lowered her eyes, her hands clasped together tightly and lying in her lap. "No. Catfish is fine. So is iced tea."

As soon as the waitress left, Tyler asked, "What's wrong?"

"Nothing."

"Bull," he mouthed. "Something's bothering

you. Either I upset you or she did. Common sense tells me it had to be me. Now, give. What did I do?"

"Well, if you really want to know, I can order my own dinner. I don't like to be bullied."

Confounded, he rocked back in the chair until his shoulders bumped the wall behind them. "Bullied?"

"Well, what would you call it?"

"How about courtesy? Or polite consideration? Maybe I was trying to be nice and take good care of you?" Judging by the confused look in Kara's eyes, he was making headway so he pressed on. "It's only bullying if I refuse to listen to your opinion, to consider your feelings. It doesn't matter whether we're discussing what to have for dinner or how to save the world. The principles are the same. You talk. I listen. Then I talk and you do the same for me. We don't have to agree. All we have to do is give each other a chance to speak honestly."

Fighting to keep the outer corners of her mouth from turning up, she asked, "May I speak honestly, right now?"

"Of course."

"Do you have any idea how *pompous* you just sounded?"

"No. Is it my turn?" Tyler waited for her nod of agreement, then continued, "Do *you* have any idea how hard it is to read your moods? They change faster than the weather in Arkansas, and that's infamous for its instability."

"Thanks."

"I didn't mean to be derogatory. I want some help, here. Talk to me, Kara. I won't bite your head off."

"Oh, yeah? Promise?" She didn't give him a chance to reply. "I suppose that's part of the problem. Every once in a while you do or say something that reminds me of Alex and I have a strong reaction to that. To you. I can't help myself. He used to pretty much manage my life—and my work—for me. I didn't like it any better then than I do now. The difference was, he *did* bite my head off if I even acted like I might object to his decisions."

Kara let herself smile and shook her head, remembering. "Face it, Tyler. I'm warped."

"Then the problem isn't me."

Rather than reveal more, she answered, "In this case, I think we can safely say no. However, you're far from perfect, in spite of what Louise and Susan keep telling me."

He placed his hand over his heart and sighed with a melodramatic air. "I'm *not* perfect? Oh, no!"

"Stop that." She elbowed him hard in the ribs. "People are staring."

"Only because we're such an imperfect pair." He purposely rubbed the side opposite to the one she'd hit, to tease her. "Ouch. That hurt when you poked me."

There was no way Kara could miss getting the joke. "I poked your *other* side, Tyler. If you don't learn your right from your left pretty soon, I don't know what I'm going to do with you.'' The instant the shortsighted words were out of her mouth, she wished she hadn't uttered them. They made her think of the future and Tyler Corbett at the same time; a dangerous concept if she'd ever heard one.

"I think I'm teachable," he said lightly. "For instance, I know that this shirt pocket is on the left side." Patting it for emphasis, he felt the paper inside. "Which reminds me..." Drawing it out, he unfolded it on the table between them and leaned closer with one arm casually draped across the back of Kara's chair. "I managed to add a few more things to my list and made a copy for you. See how it grabs you."

The lined yellow paper was there, all right. She was sure of that. And there was writing on it. Beyond that, she was at a loss. Everything was a blur. Her senses were so inundated, so overwhelmed by Tyler's nearness, the room might as well have been pitch-black. She felt the warmth of his breath on her cheek as he spoke.

"I tried to be fair and to put myself in your place, too. Most of these ideas came to me at night, while I was trying to fall asleep." His breath became a silent sigh. "I have a lot of trouble with insomnia."

"Me, too," she managed to say.

"Since you've been alone?"

"Not entirely." Tyler's presence offered enough sense of sanctuary to allow Kara to explain further. "Most of my worst nights were when I was married." She felt him tense, perceived the faint tightening of his arm around her shoulders, offering protection from a threat that no longer existed.

It didn't matter to Kara that Tyler's concern for her welfare came too late. It still warmed her heart.

Chapter Twelve

"**Y**ou should have married the first guy you proposed to," Tyler said, later.

"What are you talking about?" Kara paused with a crispy, round hushpuppy halfway to her mouth and peered up at him. "I never proposed to anybody."

"Sure, you did. Remember the zoo expert on television? Susan said you were six years old when you wrote and offered to marry him. You volunteered to take care of all his animals for him, too."

Kara's cheeks flushed pink. "So *that's* the secret Susan blabbed! Well, it's true. I didn't know how to spell some of the words in my letter, though, so I asked my big sister for help. Naturally, she couldn't keep a secret. Not about something as crazy as that. She told Mom what I was doing and I got in trouble." Kara bit into the hot hushpuppy.

"Mmm. Delicious. I love the onion flavor with the cornmeal."

"Me, too." Tyler ate one off his own plate, then asked, "What made you decide you wanted to marry some old, gray-haired geezer?"

"That's easy. I thought all those exotic animals he showed on his TV program were his personal pets and I wanted desperately to live in a wonderful household like that. I could picture dozens of wild creatures running free in every room." She laughed at herself, remembering her childish zeal. "It never occurred to me that they'd probably eat each other the first chance they got!"

Tyler concentrated on his meal for several minutes before he made up his mind to ask, "Is that why you married somebody like Alex Shepherd? Was it his connection with veterinary medicine that appealed to you?"

Kara finished the bite of deep-fried catfish she was eating, then blotted her lips with her napkin to delay answering. Finally, she spoke. "In retrospect, I suppose that was part of it. Alex and I met in vet school. At that time he seemed like a very compassionate man." And I really didn't want to go back to my parents' home and listen to more of my mother's unfair assertions about my father's death, she added to herself, pushing her plate away.

"Hey, don't let my stupid questions spoil your dinner," Tyler said solemnly.

"I wasn't as hungry as I thought, that's all."

"What have you eaten so far, today?"

"I don't know. A little of this, a little of that."

"Uh-huh. The brownie in your desk drawer?"

She was surprised he remembered. "Nope. That's long gone. I suspect Susan grabbed it when I wasn't looking. Either that, or the mice are getting big enough to open and close drawers. If that's the case, we're *all* in trouble."

"Right." Tyler returned to his dinner, eating automatically. He didn't know why, but he'd begun to worry about every aspect of Kara's daily life. Was she eating right? Had she gotten enough sleep? Was she capable of handling her largest patients without getting hurt? Was she coping okay financially?

In the back of his mind lurked additional questions he knew he'd never ask. For instance, had she known how Alex ran their joint practice, yet kept quiet, condoning his unscrupulous methods by her silence? Had she been so intimidated by the man that she'd abandoned the strong code of ethics which now seemed to govern her work; her life?

He didn't want to believe any of that about Kara. He didn't want to…but he did.

Tyler got home to find Mark sitting on his front porch, waiting for him.

Weary, he raised both hands in surrender. "Don't worry. You can tell your wife I never laid a hand on her sister."

"Did Kara lay anything on you?"

"Yeah. A guilt trip," Tyler said. "Just about the time I think we understand each other, she starts acting moody all over again. I can't figure her out."

"Do you have to? Figure her out, I mean."

Poking the brim of his Western hat with one finger to tilt it back on his head, Tyler propped his booted foot on the step beside Mark and leaned against a porch post, mulling over the question. "I'm not sure. It's like Kara needs me. I don't mean in the usual sense, man to woman, I mean something deeper."

Mark shrugged and shook his head. "I won't pretend to know what you're talking about. But then, I've never lost anybody who was close to me the way you two have. Maybe that's it. Maybe Kara senses that you know how she feels."

"Except half the time I don't," Tyler admitted ruefully. "It's as if she's two different people. She can be so moody she drives me crazy, or so playful we wind up having fun together. To tell you the truth, it scares me."

Chuckling low, Mark got to his feet. "Sounds to me like everything is normal. That alone is a miracle. Susan says Kara hardly ever used to cut loose and have a good time when they were kids. She kept to herself a lot, studying or reading or doctoring some stray animal and trying to keep it hidden in her room so their father wouldn't see it and blow his stack."

"That reminds me. What else can you tell me

about his death?'' Pausing for a moment, Tyler guessed, ''It had something to do with Kara, didn't it?''

Mark nodded. ''Maybe. In a roundabout way. She'd brought home an abused horse, of all things, and stashed it in the garage. Her father heard a noise, opened the garage door, and came face-to-face with the poor old nag. He yelled at Kara till his blood pressure was probably going through the roof. A couple hours later he had his first stroke.''

''First stroke? He didn't die then?''

''No. But he wound up paralyzed on one side. Susan tried to smooth things over with their mother. It didn't work. Kara got all the blame for him being stuck in a wheelchair.''

Tyler's heart went out to the altruistic young woman. ''How old was she then?''

''Let's see…'' Mark thought for a few seconds. ''It was after Susan and I got married. Kara must have been almost eighteen. She won a scholarship and went away to college that summer.''

''And married Alex Shepherd.''

''Not right away. Vets have to have as much training as MDs. She met Alex when she finished college and started in the veterinary program at Purdue.''

Tyler took off his hat and raked his fingers through his hair, combing it back while he pondered what he'd just learned and tried to put it into logical perspective. Except for Susan and Mark, it looked like Kara had no family to rely on, no one else to support her emotionally and help her heal. No wonder she was still suffering so.

The more he thought about it, the more Tyler began to see the Lord's hand in what was currently taking place. Kara just needed someone to lean on for a little while. Someone who understood what she'd been through. Someone to show her that no one could change the past, no matter how hard they prayed or how much they wished things had turned out differently.

Someone who had cursed and shouted at God for what had happened to Dee—and still been forgiven.

Someone like him.

Kara had tucked Tyler's list in her purse. As soon as she got home, she kicked off her shoes, brewed a cup of hot chocolate, curled up in the corner of her sofa with Speedy at her feet, and unfolded the paper.

It started out predictably with, "no kissing," then progressed to, "no unnecessary hugging." So far, so good.

Below that, he'd made two columns. The one on the left was headed with a big, Yes. Kara scanned that, first. It listed teasing, winking, squirting with a hose, sneaking out of church, sharing a busted-up dog, eating cold pizza, acting silly and kissing behind the barn. He'd crossed out the part about kissing but left enough of it showing that she could tell what had been written there.

Chuckling to herself, Kara took a small sip of her hot chocolate and started to read the No column. She nearly strangled. Gasping, she blew chocolate all over her lap, peppering the yellow paper. The first items dealt with neck and ear nibbling! After that, the list got even more ridiculous, including rolling in the hay and eloping! Why couldn't the man ever be serious?

As soon as she got her coughing under control, she grabbed the telephone directory and dialed his number, not caring how late it was.

Tyler answered on the third ring. "If you're selling something, go away. I'm beat."

"I'm not selling, and I'm not *giving* anything away, either. I'm not that kind of woman, in spite of what you seem to think."

"Ah." He was laughing. "Who is this? Could it be the cute little vet who dumped a mutt on my doorstep?"

"You know very well who it is," Kara said. His comment about her being cute was pleasing but she wasn't too thrilled with the *little* reference.

"I take it you finally got around to actually reading my list. I wondered why you took it so calmly when I showed it to you when we were at Bea's."

"This is not funny, Tyler."

"Sure, it is. Give yourself time. You'll eventually see the humor."

Unfortunately, she already did. Stifling a giggle, she pantomimed an exaggerated look of disdain at the telephone in place of scowling at him in person. "Did you really think it was necessary to tell me *not* to do all those things?"

"I don't know. Was it?" He heard her muffled, predictable grumbling and broke into loud laughter. Getting control of himself he finally said, "Okay, okay. I'm sorry. I know you'd never elope with me. Not even if I promised to take you all the way to Tahiti."

"That's right, mister. Go find yourself another pretend girlfriend. I quit."

"Uh-oh. I think we're having our first lovers' quarrel."

Kara was really having trouble sounding mad. She couldn't think of the right words to express her supposed anger. "Tyler Corbett, you are the most..."

"Yes? Go on. I'm all ears."

"You're all *something,* all right, but it isn't ears," she retorted. There was no way to hide the smile in her voice or her delight with the absurd conversation they were having. "I'll fix the list and have it ready the next time I see you."

"Well, okay, but leave the part about no neck nibbling in public. I have a reputation to protect, you know."

That did it. Kara managed to hang up the receiver moments before bursting into giggles. Reacting to her upbeat mood, Speedy jumped halfway into her lap, eager to share in the fun.

She hugged him, speaking as if he could understand every word. "Oh, that Tyler Corbett. He's a...a..." Describing the situation rationally, even when talking to a dog, was impossible. The things about Tyler that kept coming to mind were so complimentary they were embarrassing. Visualizing his kind face gave her a peace she'd never known. His sparkling gaze blessed her all the way to her soul, even when he wasn't smiling. And that smile! It warmed her all the way to her toes. Half the time it made her feel like she was floating.

"Know what the best part about him is, Speedy?" Kara cupped the dog's narrow face in her hands and held him still so she could look into his eyes as she spoke. "The man makes me laugh. Really, truly laugh. I don't remember ever feeling this way before."

The greyhound's tongue shot out, aiming for her face, but Kara was too quick for him. "Oh, no, you don't. No face licking." She giggled. "Would you believe it? That's on his goofy list, too!"

Kara's bedside phone rang just before dawn. Groggy, she answered with a slurred, "Hello?"

"Kara. It's me. Tyler."

"Mmm. If you think it's funny to wake me up like this, just because I called you so late last night, you're wrong. I'm not laughing. Bye, Tyler." She started to replace the receiver, heard him shout, and brought it back to her ear. "What is it? Is Susan okay?"

There was profound sadness in his voice. "Susan's fine. It's Buster. I went to let him outside this morning, just like I always do, and when he tried to get up, he couldn't walk."

Kara was suddenly wide-awake. She sat up in bed. "No other symptoms?"

"Not that I can tell. He's been eating well and hasn't seemed run down or sick. I thought maybe he had a muscle cramp or something like that, so I lifted him into a standing position. He collapsed the minute I let go."

"How about his pupils? Are they equal and reactive?" She rephrased. "I mean, do they both dilate at the same speed and look the same size?"

"I don't know. Hang on. I'll check."

While Tyler was away from the phone, Kara quickly began to dress. She had the receiver tucked between her ear and shoulder and was fastening her jeans when he returned.

"It's hard to tell for sure. I think both his eyes look the same," Tyler said, breathless. "What should I do?"

Kara hesitated for a moment, praying the problem wasn't serious. "If you can carry him to your truck without hurting him, it would be best if I saw him at the office so I have all my equipment handy in case I need it."

"I'll get him there. Just say when."

"I live out on Peace Valley Road. It'll be driving time from here to Hardy. I'm leaving right away."

"Okay. We'll meet you there."

Kara headed for the door, hopping on one foot while she tried to slip her other foot into a sandal. The fact that Tyler had called her for help was pretty profound, considering his former negative opinion of her practice. She didn't even want to think about how he'd feel—how she'd feel—if poor old Buster didn't pull through.

Tyler was waiting when Kara arrived. She skidded her truck to a stop next to his and leaped out. "Where is he?"

"Here. On the front seat," Tyler said, opening the door wider. "He seemed happy to be taken for a ride, even if I did have to lift him into the truck."

"Oh, good." Kara let the dog sniff her hand, then began to systematically touch his whole body, beginning at his head. When she got to his hips, he winced.

Tyler crowded in behind her to watch. "What is it?"

"Probably an injury. Maybe hip dysplasia. I can't tell without an X ray. He wasn't showing signs of breaking down when I saw him in your kitchen with Roady, so I suspect he just hurt himself."

"Will he be okay?"

The poignant note in Tyler's voice touched Kara

all the way to her soul. If there was ever a time she needed to pull off a miracle, it was now. Keeping one hand on Buster so he wouldn't try to move and make things worse, she looked up into the man's eyes and spoke honestly. "I think he'll be fine. But no one can give you a positive guarantee about something like this. All I can say is that I've had a lot of experience with big dogs and I'll do my best to help him."

"That's all I ask," Tyler said soberly. "Is there anything I can do?"

"Yes. You can carry him inside for me as soon as I unlock the door and get an exam room ready."

"Of course. Anything else?"

She thought about how she'd been asking the Lord for help ever since Tyler's call had awakened her. "Well, I don't think it's against any rules to pray for a pet."

"If it is, it shouldn't be."

Kara saw the beginnings of a smile lift the corners of his mouth and her heart warmed. This was why she'd gone into veterinary medicine in the first place; to help animals and to soothe the people who loved them. Expressions of her personal faith didn't always fit the situation but she didn't hide her beliefs, either. In a case like Tyler's, where she knew how he felt, she saw no reason not to include God in the equation.

"I'm glad to see you're feeling better," Kara said

kindly. "If you're upset, Buster will pick up on your mood and he'll worry, too."

"I hate to imagine what he was thinking when I found him, then. He sure scared me."

Kara laid her hand lightly on his arm. "I understand. I know how special he is to you." With a little smile, she added, "And I'm flattered that you brought him to me. Just wait here a minute. I'll come back and get you when I have everything ready."

Tyler's jaw went slack as he watched Kara unlock the door and disappear inside. When she'd said she was flattered to be chosen, he'd realized that he hadn't even considered looking for a different vet. He'd found Buster ailing, panicked, and immediately called Kara, as if she were the only one qualified to help.

And she'd responded exactly as he'd known she would. Promptly and without reservation.

Buster was panting. Tyler stroked his side and spoke softly to help keep him calm. "I don't know whether you look better because you liked the ride over here, or if you just wanted to come see Kara again. Either way, you scared me silly, you know that?"

The golden Labrador thumped his tail and looked at his master as if he understood every word.

"Yeah, I know what you mean. I feel better now that we're here, too. There is something special about Kara, isn't there? You wouldn't happen to know what that special something is, would you old pal?''

Buster cocked his head, looking supremely intelligent but remaining silent.

''No, I didn't think you would. You're every bit as bumfuzzled by her as I am, aren't you? There are times when she really gets to me.''

Tyler broke off. He didn't even want to contemplate the possible significance of what he'd just admitted. ''Thank goodness you can't talk the way those dogs in the TV commercials do,'' he told Buster. ''I could be in real trouble if you told anybody what I just said.''

Chapter Thirteen

Tyler was an emotional wreck by the time Kara had finished X-raying and treating Buster.

"He'll be groggy for a while," she said as she and Tyler slid the dog into a small holding cage to keep him from moving around too much. "He needs to be kept inactive until the anesthetic wears off. I don't want him trying to get up and falling."

"You're sure it's not serious?"

"Like I said, his hip snapped back into its socket when we stretched him out for the X-ray. There's very little sign of wear on the joint, so it should stay in place. I'll give him some muscle relaxants and painkillers when he's fully conscious. You should be able to take him home late this afternoon."

Tyler exhaled in a noisy whoosh. "Okay. Thanks."

"You're both quite welcome." Pleased, she checked the wall clock. "Uh-oh. I need to get going."

"Why? You're already at work."

"True. But I didn't let Speedy out or feed any of my other animals before I left home."

"I could go feed them for you. That is, if I knew where in Peace Valley you lived."

"You could," she said, starting for the door, "but it might cost you an arm or a leg. I'm not sure how Harry and Peewee would react to a stranger on their turf, especially when I'm not there. And I'm sure Whiskers would go after you, even though he isn't big enough to do much damage, which would probably inspire the other dogs to follow his lead."

"Then at least let me drive you home."

Kara grinned up at him. "My, my. You are a brave man, aren't you?"

"I'm wearing my cowboy boots," he countered, holding out one foot. "Anything that tries to bite my ankles will hit leather."

"How high, exactly, do those boots go?" she asked, giggling. "Whiskers is a little terrier-mix, but Harry's part German shepherd."

"What's Peewee? Or shouldn't I ask?"

"Well..." She was getting a kick out of the guarded look on his handsome face. "Tell you what. Why don't I take you up on your offer of a ride and let you see for yourself?"

"That big, huh?"

"Don't say I didn't warn you."

Peewee was first to bound up to greet Tyler's truck. The other dogs followed. Several gray-striped cats watched cautiously from the sidelines.

Tyler slowed to avoid the boisterous lead dog. "What is *that?* Wait. Let me guess. That's Peewee?"

"You've got it. As near as I can tell, he's part Rottweiler, part brindle Great Dane, and part fence jumper."

"He looks more like a man-eater. Reminds me of how I always used to picture the hound of the Baskervilles when I was a kid."

"My favorite books were the ones about Irish Setters and sled dogs," Kara said. "And Lassie, of course. For years, I begged my parents to get me a collie."

"Do you have one of those, too?"

"No." Talking to her dogs to calm them, she climbed down from Tyler's truck and was instantly surrounded by the affectionate pack. She spoke to each dog and gave it a pat before she looked back at Tyler. "Purebreds are wonderful, of course. There are just too many strays in need of a home for me to go looking for another dog. As you can see, I have plenty already."

"No kidding. Think they'll let me get out, now? I know they haven't had any breakfast yet. I'd hate to be their first course."

Chuckling softly, Kara took hold of Peewee's collar and told him to sit. The other dogs did, as well, although the brown-and-white terrier was so excited he had trouble staying in one place. They all looked to their mistress for further instruction.

"I'd like you to meet Mr. Corbett, guys," she said to them. "He's okay. Well, sort of okay. He likes animals so he can't be all bad."

"Oh, that was a wonderful introduction. Now they *will* eat me," Tyler said with a mock scowl.

"It's my tone of voice more than my words that they pick up on, and you know it. I could tell them you were the dogcatcher and they'd still welcome you if I said it with love."

"Is that where they all came from? Animal control, I mean." He slowly opened the truck door and put one foot on the ground.

"Mostly. Each one has its own sad story. Speedy used to be a racing dog. The others were basically throwaways."

Tyler joined her, letting the dogs sniff his jeans and boots before chancing to offer a hand. "Which one is Speedy?"

"He's still in the house," Kara said. "Come on." Satisfied that Tyler had been accepted, she released her hold on the largest dog and started to walk away. The whole group tagged along at her heels, Tyler included.

"I feel like I'm in a parade," he joked. "Is it

always like this around here or are they just hungry?"

"They're my friends. When you make the rounds at your ranch, don't you take Buster with you?"

"Not much anymore," Tyler said pensively. "I used to. Then I started leaving him in the house because Dee didn't want to be alone. I just never started taking him with me again, after..."

"You don't have to explain. I think he'd benefit from daily exercise, though, once he's back on his feet. You might consider it."

"I will." Watching her open the front door without unlocking it, he asked, "Do you always go away and leave the place wide-open?"

Kara laughed again and pointed to her pack of furry escorts. "If you were a burglar, would you come here?"

"Not on your life!" The thought made him grin. "One look would be enough to end my criminal career for good." Following her into the living room, he was greeted by a flash of tan and white that leaped at him like a specter, landed with its front paws on his shoulders long enough to give him a kiss, then got down and spun in circles at his feet. Tyler stifled a yell of surprise and stood his ground.

"That's Speedy, in case you haven't guessed," Kara said. "He's very friendly. He's also very fast in comparison to my other dogs. For a greyhound, he wasn't all that speedy, though. That's why his owners stopped racing him."

"Judging by the look on your face, Speedy was one of the lucky ones. What usually happens to them when their racing days are over?"

"You don't want to know," Kara said. "If I had all the money in the world, I'd probably spend it taking care of the unwanted pets that had been shoved out on the street to fend for themselves." Thinking about how close she'd come to losing everything after Alex had died and left her saddled with a pile of debts she didn't know about, she shivered. As long as her veterinary practice continued to grow, she'd be okay. But one hiccup in the normal operations and she could still lose everything she'd worked so hard for.

Tyler noticed the negative shift in her mood and tried to change it for the better. "I can see it now," he teased. "The Kara Shepherd Home for Elderly Animals. Our motto is, 'You shove 'em, we love 'em.' How does that sound?"

"About as ridiculous as you meant it to." She sent a smile his way. "Thanks. Once I get on my soapbox there's no telling what I'll say."

He reached for her hand, relieved when Speedy didn't object. "There's no reason to be ashamed of caring about injustices or for trying to put some of them right. Just because you can't cure all the world's ills, doesn't mean you shouldn't want to. The way I see it, when you're led to the special ones you can help, you just do what you can. That's all anyone can ask."

Kara looked into his eyes and saw an empathy equal to hers that took her breath away. This man did understand what she was trying to do. And why she'd never stop. His touch was warm and strong, but more important, it was compassionate. Without that remarkable quality, holding his hand would mean little. With it, his touch was momentous.

Sighing, she laid her free hand on top of his as he continued to gently clasp her fingers. She had no doubt she was supposed to help the lost, lonely animals that crossed her path. But what about the lonely people? What about this man in particular? Had she been led to him? Or, worse, had they been led to each other?

Oh, Father, Kara prayed silently. *Not me. Not yet. I'm not ready for this. Besides, I'm a veterinarian, not a social worker.*

Tell me you're not lonely, a voice inside her said.

She tightened her grip on Tyler's hand. Mere seconds had passed since he'd reached for her, yet it seemed as if they'd been standing there for an eternity.

I'd rather be lonely, she insisted. *I tried marriage. Anything is better than that.*

Kara felt, rather than heard, echos of rich, wholesome laughter. Her eyes widened.

"What's wrong?" Tyler dropped her hand and scanned the room in the direction of her anxious gaze.

"I thought I heard something." She humphed in

disgust. "Never mind. It was probably just God, laughing at me." Before Tyler could comment, she added, "I always did think the Lord had a sense of humor. He'd have to, dealing with us."

"Us, as in mankind? Or, us, as in you and me?"

"Take your pick," Kara said. Starting for the kitchen, she added, "Come on. You can open cans for me."

Tyler considered her house as he followed. The living room was neat but sparsely decorated. Larger pieces of furniture, such as a sofa and chairs were present. What was missing were the smaller objects, like lamps, knickknacks, end tables and anything that might be breakable. Considering the way Speedy raced around the house leaping over anything in his path, that was understandable. Whatever Kara hadn't removed to start with had probably been broken the minute the dog had arrived.

Her old-fashioned kitchen was a pleasant surprise. Tyler paused and began to grin. "Wow. This looks just like my grandma's kitchen when I was a boy. She even had a Hoosier cabinet like that." Reminiscing, he ran his hand over the well-used, white-painted finish of the upright, freestanding cupboard. "If I remember right, this enamel countertop slides out."

"I was lucky to find one that still works," Kara said. "Most of them have been altered to fit into modern kitchens where nobody cares about function the way folks used to. That one even has the flour bin still in it. Go ahead. Take a look." She was pleased to see he felt enough at home to open the upper compartments as she'd suggested. Truth to tell, he seemed more relaxed in her kitchen than he had in his own house.

Tyler turned to her. "Do you bake?"

"Occasionally. When I get the urge. I'm afraid the cabinet doesn't get the regular workout it did in the old days, though. It's hard to imagine having to bake enough bread and pastries to feed a whole family."

Watching her line up the dog's dishes, he chuckled. "In your case, it shouldn't be too hard. Everybody in your family eats off the floor!"

"True." Kara wasn't at all put off by his candid remark. "And they're not fussy." She set two large cans on the counter beside her.

Tyler took them. "I'll open these. What else?"

"That's it for the morning meal. I sure wish I could leave dry food out all the time but the dogs are so lazy they let the raccoons and possums steal it if I do." She was going to mention the added cost of feeding wild creatures as well as her own animals, then thought better of it. Considering the way he'd acted the last time Susan had billed him, the less she and Tyler discussed the specifics of their personal finances, the better off they'd be.

Mulling over their past conflicts, Kara led the way into the backyard. Now that she was getting to know Tyler better she had serious doubts he'd have withheld payment of a bona fide debt. Yet that was what he'd apparently done, judging by the information she'd been able to glean from Alex's records.

Doing her chores automatically while her imagination churned out one unbelievable idea after another, Kara fed the dogs, put cat food up on a high, secure ledge so the cats could eat in peace, then threw a fresh flake of hay to the old carriage horse and made sure all the water troughs and buckets were filled.

By the time she was through she'd decided what to do. Somehow, she was going to find out what had actually gone wrong after Alex had vaccinated the Corbett herd, even if it meant she had to personally go through every scrap of paper and every supplier's bill in the boxes and boxes of disorganized files she'd put into storage after Alex's death. The answer must be there somewhere.

All she had to do was find it.

Buster was sitting in his cage looking fairly alert by the time Tyler returned Kara to the animal hospital. Susan was already at work. She started to greet Kara, saw Tyler with her, and froze, speechless.

"Good morning to you, too," Kara teased. "What's the matter? Cat got your tongue?"

"You could say that." Susan grabbed her arm and pulled her aside. "Where did *he* come from?"

"Texas, originally, I think. Why?"

"Stop that. I'm not kidding. When I got here, saw

your truck out front and couldn't locate you, I was worried sick.''

"I left you a note. At least I think I did. I know I meant to.''

"But you had other things on your mind, right?'' She nodded toward Tyler. "Him, for instance.''

"Buster was sick. Tyler called and I came in early. That's all there was to it.''

"Uh-huh. If I hadn't recognized Tyler's dog in the recovery area, I'd have probably called the police and reported you missing.''

Tyler stepped up and joined the conversation. "It was my fault, Susan. Buster couldn't walk. I panicked. I only drove your sister home so I could help her with her morning chores. I figured that was fair, since I was the reason she hadn't stopped to do them before she left.''

Susan was not about to be placated. "I don't care if you two decide to elope to Las Vegas,'' she declared, hands on her hips, "I would like to be told what's going on if Kara decides to disappear, again.''

In unison, Kara and Tyler both said, "Tahiti,'' then shared a chuckle at the private joke.

Finally, Kara looped an arm around her sister's shoulders and started to lead her away. "Come on. I'll tell you all about my adventure while we get ready to open.''

"You'd better,'' Susan warned, scowling.

Kara glanced back over her shoulder and called,

"Thanks for your help. You can come back for Buster this afternoon."

"Okay. See you then." Tyler tipped his hat and left.

As soon as the door closed behind him Kara let her exhaustion show. "Whew."

Susan immediately softened. "Are you sick?" She put her hand on her sister's brow. "You don't have a fever."

"No, I'm not sick. At least not the way you mean. I just can't seem to shake off an absurd compulsion to find out what actually happened to Tyler's cattle, back when Alex was treating them. Maybe the vaccine was bad. Or maybe the lab made a mistake on the tests we ran. I don't know. Something."

"Why bother? That was years ago. What difference will it make at this late date?"

"It makes a difference to me."

Susan was slowly shaking her head. "You may be sorry if you go digging into the past. What you find out could change the way Tyler feels about you."

Kara opened her mouth to say she didn't care, then realized the opposite was true. She did care. But only because they'd become such good friends. She trusted him and she knew he trusted her. That element of their relationship meant she owed him the absolute truth, no matter what it was. And if her search proved her business blameless in his misfortune, as she believed it would, they'd no longer have an outdated suspicion standing between them.

"I have to know," Kara finally said, starting for her office. "For my sake as much as for Tyler's."

Susan followed. "And if the whole thing was Alex's fault? What then?"

"It can't have been. Alex wasn't perfect but he was a good vet. Smart and capable."

"And honest?"

Kara froze. Her head snapped around. "Is there some problem with the books you haven't told me about?"

"Nothing I can't fix," Susan said. "You may have to go back and file an amended tax return for the last couple of years you were married, though. Alex was pretty creative when he made out the original forms he had you sign."

"Oh, wonderful. I suppose that means I'll owe the government more money."

"Probably. But maybe we can average your income and break even. I'll give it a try. In the meantime, I don't suppose you'd like me to try to collect on any more bills that are years past due, would you?"

"Who's on that list besides Tyler Corbett?" Kara asked, anticipating the answer.

Susan merely shrugged and smiled sweetly. "Never mind. Bad idea." She quickly spun around and headed for the reception area. "Guess I'd better get back to work."

Watching her go, Kara thanked God for her sister's loving presence and willingness to share her skills. Without Susan's proficient management there would have been no way Kara could have kept the animal hospital going. Alex had left the books so jumbled it had taken a professional like Susan to make any sense of them.

A shiver of foreboding skittered up Kara's spine like the delicate scamper of tiny, invisible mouse paws. "Alex was just disorganized," she countered aloud. "That's all. As soon as I find the original records I'll be able to prove he had nothing to do with Tyler's terrible losses."

In her subconscious, however, lingering disquiet refused to be banished. Kara knew she'd have no real peace until she sought out the truth.

Chapter Fourteen

Buster was more than ready to go home by closing time. Kara delayed leaving work, expecting Tyler to come for his dog, as he'd promised.

She walked into the front office just as Susan was hanging up the telephone. "I just called the ranch. Mark says they had an emergency with one of the horses and lost track of time. I'm supposed to give Buster a ride home."

"That'll be fine. You told him you would, didn't you?"

"Actually, no." Susan displayed a self-satisfied smile. "I'm planning to buy a lot of groceries after work. My car will be way too full. Guess you'll have to do the honors."

"Susan..."

"Hey, don't look at me. I'm just the messenger."

"Then we'll trade vehicles. You take my truck. Put Buster in the front with you and load all your groceries in the back."

"What if it rains?"

Kara was getting frustrated. "It's *not* going to rain." She marched through the reception area to the glassed-in front. "There's not a cloud in the…" The instant she peered out, she realized her flawless rationale was no longer valid. "Okay, so there are a few clouds. That doesn't mean a thing in Arkansas. It might not rain for a month."

"Or it might rain right away and ruin my groceries before I can drive home. Sorry. The way I see it, you have two choices. You can either take Buster to the ranch yourself, or leave him here, alone in that cramped, little cage, all night long."

Kara pulled a face. "You know I'd never subject an animal to unnecessary confinement."

The older sister shrugged. "Whatever. Like I said, it's up to you. I'm sure Tyler will understand why Mark couldn't manage to arrange to have Buster brought home." She retrieved her purse from the lowest drawer of her desk and slung the slim strap over one shoulder. "Well, gotta go. See you tomorrow."

Kara's plea of, "Hey, wait!" was fruitless. Susan had already ducked out the door. "I'll get you for this," she muttered, stomping off toward the kennel area. "You knew just how to get to me, didn't you?" Her voice mimicked her sister's, "*Poor dog, alone all night.* And when that didn't work, you brought up Mark's obligations to his boss. Talk about great strategy!''

Buster wagged his tail happily when Kara leaned down to unlatch his cage. Speaking softly, she petted and reassured him as she snapped a leash to the ring on his collar and started to lead him carefully across the concrete floor. "That's it, old boy. Take it easy. You'll be fine." Her tone never changed as she continued, "Of course, *I* may wind up a basket case if I hang around your owner much more, but nobody seems to care about that. No, sir. They sure don't. They just throw Tyler and me together and watch the fur fly."

She locked the door and walked to her truck, the yellow Lab ambling along beside her. Rather than encourage him to jump in when she opened the truck door, she placed his front feet on the floor of the cab, then eased his rear end in by lifting it herself so he wouldn't further injure himself. If he'd been much heavier—or much lazier—she couldn't have accomplished the task without help.

By the time she'd circled the truck to climb behind the wheel, Buster was lounging on the seat, looking terribly pleased with himself. He was panting, his wide, pink tongue lolling out the side of his mouth.

Kara laughed and ruffled his velvety ears. "You old faker. You aren't having a bit of trouble getting around, are you? I'll bet your daddy will really be relieved.''

The thought of Tyler's reaction to her use of that silly nickname made her smile. Come to think of it, so did everything else about the man, from the color of his hair, to the mischievous sparkle in his eyes, to the warm, reassuring feel of his hand when it touched hers.

Sighing, she realized she was beginning to feel a lot like a teenager experiencing love for the first time. At least she thought she was. Her younger years hadn't been particularly enlightening where romantic relationships were concerned. There was a good chance she was merely imagining what falling in love would be like.

That conclusion brought her up short. Surely, she'd loved Alex once. She must have. After all, she'd married the man! But she'd never noticed thinking about him all the time. Or worrying if he was okay. Or constantly reliving their time together.

With Tyler, she'd done all those things. She hadn't wanted him to become such an integral part of her life; she simply couldn't stop her subconscious from dwelling on the joy and peace that blessed her whenever he was near. Lately, all she had to do was remember being with him and a similar awareness flowed through her, soothing away her hidden fears and calming her jumbled emotions.

''Oh, Buster,'' Kara crooned, laying her hand on the dog's broad head for mutual comfort. ''I think

I'm in big trouble. Your daddy is starting to look far too good to me. And I have absolutely no idea what I should do about it."

Kara saw Mark standing by the barn when she arrived at the ranch, so she drove straight to him.

"I brought Buster," she said, leaning out the truck window. "Will you lift him down for me? I don't want him to jump yet."

"Sure." As soon as the dog was firmly on the ground, Mark straightened, dusted his hands on his jeans, and cocked his head toward the open barn door. "Ty's in the foaling stall down at the far end. We had a colt coming breach and had to pull it."

"Are the mare and the foal both all right?" Kara asked.

"Just fine. I was about to head for the house for dinner. You staying?"

Her brow knit. "I beg your pardon? I thought Susan was going grocery shopping after work."

Mark shrugged. "First I've heard of it. I saw her drive in a few minutes ago." He looked down at the dog. "Hey, why didn't you have her bring Buster home? Would have saved you a trip."

"I know." Kara's voice oozed pseudosweetness. "I guess I got confused." She handed the looped end of the leash to her brother-in-law. "Here. You do the honors. Just warn Tyler to keep him fairly quiet for a few more days and he should be fine."

"Okay, but…"

"Thanks. And don't hurry home. Okay? I want time to have a nice, private, sisterly talk with your wife."

Kara got back in her truck and took off, wheels spinning, leaving Mark behind in a cloud of dust. By the time she reached Susan's she'd managed to think of more than one choice comment to express her displeasure. When she barged into the kitchen, however, her sister grabbed her hands and greeted her with such delight it floored her.

"So, how did it go? Was he impressed that you went to all the trouble of bringing his dog home? He sure should have been. For a minute there I was afraid you weren't going to take advantage of the opportunity."

"Opportunity?" Kara said, confused.

"Sure! You've been playing too hard to get. I mean, the man did bring you his favorite dog when he could have taken it to another vet. How much more does he have to do to convince you he likes you?"

"Of course he likes me. We're friends...well, sort of. I like him, too."

Susan cheered. "Yeah! About time. I was beginning to think you'd never stop brooding."

"I don't brood," Kara argued. "I just don't dance around the room when something pleases me."

"Not anymore, maybe, but you used to. Don't you remember when we put on that talent show in the backyard? I was a clown. You were a ballerina.

And we'd organized the other kids in the neighborhood into our stage crew.'' Her smile grew wistful. ''Mom and Dad laughed and applauded so hard I thought they were going to fall off their seats.''

Kara spoke softly, sadly. ''I don't remember it happening that way.''

''That's because you always take things too seriously. We all had a wonderful time.''

''Till our father lost his temper, started yelling, and the other kids all went home.''

Leading her to the kitchen table, Susan pushed her gently into a chair, then pulled another one close. ''You don't know why? You really don't?'' She shook her head when Kara didn't answer. ''It was because one of the little boys knocked you down and made you cry, then wouldn't apologize.''

''That can't be right.'' Tears began to sting Kara's eyes and blur her vision. ''Dad was always getting mad and shouting for no reason.''

''I know, honey, but you were the only one who ever took him seriously. Even Mom didn't listen when he acted like that. I suppose that's why she paid no attention to his hollering and he laid there in the driveway for so long.''

''When?''

''When he had his first stroke.''

Kara's eyes widened, spilling rivulets of tears down her cheeks. No one had ever told her that part of the story. ''It doesn't matter. He'd have been fine if I hadn't brought that old horse home and hidden it in the garage.''

''No way. Dad might have done better if he'd gotten medical attention faster, or if he'd cooperated with his physical therapist, or if he'd kept his blood pressure down and dieted like he was supposed to. But he had a volatile temper he couldn't, or wouldn't, control. That was his problem, not ours. Even Mom has finally realized she wasn't to blame for what happened.''

Kara was adamant. ''She never blamed herself, she blamed *me*. So did he. They told me so.''

''Oh, honey…'' Susan reached out and pulled her sister into a warm, forgiving hug. ''They blamed everybody at first—you, me, the doctors. Even God. But later, when they'd had a chance to accept Dad's illness, they both changed for the better. Toward the end of his life they seemed very happy. I think they even fell in love with each other again.''

Weeping, Kara clung to her sister. ''But—but they never said. They never told me. I always thought…''

''You'd moved away and finished college by the time I realized our father had finally grown up. You had a life of your own. A husband. Your career. I never dreamed you were still hurting over that stupid misunderstanding or I'd have said something sooner. I'm sure Mom would have, too.''

She reached for a box of tissues, took one for herself, then offered the rest to her sister. They blew their noses in unison. Their eyes met. Compassion and acceptance flowed between them.

Susan was the first to break into a smile. "You look awful, kid."

"Hah!" Sniffling, Kara made a silly face and blotted her tears. "You don't look so good yourself. Besides, you're older. You're supposed to look worse than I do."

"Oh, thanks a heap."

"You're welcome." She glanced toward the door as Mark entered. When he saw what was going on, the bewildered look on his face was priceless.

Coming to an abrupt halt, he held up both hands in surrender. "Oops. Sorry to intrude. Do you want me to go outside and wait until you're through?"

"Through with what?" Susan asked, sniffling. "There's no problem here, is there, Kara?"

"Nope." She felt as if an enormous burden had been lifted from her soul. All along she'd been praying that she'd be able to accept her guilt for her father's affliction and be forgiven. Instead, she'd been presented with a much better answer. There was no guilt to forgive!

Mark lingered by the door, acting as if he didn't believe their assurance that nothing momentous was taking place. "Um. Okay, I guess. If you say so."

Gazing at him fondly, his wife walked up, took his hand, and tugged him through the kitchen. When they reached the hallway she slipped into his embrace and kissed him. "Stop worrying. We were just having a little woman-to-woman talk. Those are like watching old, romantic movies. They almost always require three or four tissues.''

Observing Susan's and Mark's loving rapport as they kissed again made Kara painfully aware of how truly alone she was. She slipped out the open back door without saying goodbye so they could have some well-deserved privacy.

As she made her way to her truck, Kara realized her heart was finally at peace with regard to her parents. At least they'd found happiness before it was too late. How wonderful it would be to live in the kind of family Susan had built with Mark. All a person had to do was look at them to see they were deeply in love. Surely it wasn't covetousness to wish the same for herself.

The problem was, she kept making stupid mistakes about men. The first time, she'd been fooled by Alex's shrewd deception. This time, however, she'd walked into trouble with her eyes wide-open and fallen in love with a man who'd once enjoyed an ideal marriage, had an ideal wife. No one could ever live up to those kinds of standards. Especially not her.

Kara was so numbed by her heartbreaking conclusion she literally bumped into Tyler before she noticed him.

He caught her arm to steady her. ''Hey, Doc. Glad you're still here. I saw your truck was here so I came on over. Thanks again for what you did for Buster.''

"It's my job," she said soberly.

"Fixing his leg was your job. Giving him a ride home wasn't. Mark told you why I didn't make it back to Hardy?"

"Yes." She tried to edge past him but he was blocking the way. "I'm glad the mare and foal came through all right."

"Me, too. Which gives us a great reason to celebrate. How about letting me take you out to dinner again?"

"Not tonight."

Tyler tilted up her chin with one finger, forcing her to look at him. "Are you mad at me for some reason?"

"No." She twisted free. "I'm just tired. It's been a long day. All I want to do is go home and crash."

He knew a lame excuse when he heard one, especially since Kara was such an atrocious liar. What he didn't know was why she was putting him off. "No problem. We'll get takeout and eat it at your place. That should prove pretty challenging, considering the animals you have under foot."

"Really, Tyler, I don't feel much like celebrating."

"Okay. Have it your way." Stepping aside, he opened the truck door for her, slamming it as soon as she was settled behind the wheel. "I'll share my special dinner with Buster and Road Kill. They'll love it."

Kara purposely avoided looking at him again.

She'd been fighting additional tears ever since she'd admitted she was in love with him. All she wanted to do now was escape before she made a worse fool of herself—not that that would be easy, given the scope of her primary idiotic mistake.

Spending time with Tyler Corbett was supposed to have been a safe alternative to serious involvement for both of them. Instead, she was hopelessly in love. And he was just as hopelessly ignorant of it.

"Good thing," she muttered to herself, driving off with a brief wave instead of bidding him a normal goodbye. "If he had a clue how I felt he'd probably run so fast to get away from me he'd put Speedy to shame."

The doldrums would have been a step up for Kara that evening. She did her chores mechanically, then showered and changed into shorts and an over-size T-shirt to take full advantage of the cool night air. Lying on the sofa, she'd almost drifted off to sleep when the barking of her dogs roused her. By the time she got to the porch, the bedlam had ceased. It was easy to see why.

Tyler had backed his new pickup into her driveway. He was seated on a lawn chair in the truck bed, pitching tidbits over the side to pacify the milling pack below. He waved. "Hi, Doc. Want to join us for dinner? We're having country fried chicken."

"Stop that! You can't give dogs chicken bones," Kara shouted. "The splinters can kill them."

"I know. I bought a bucket of nuggets for them. You and I get the parts with the bones in them."

She could see how proud he was to have come up with such a unique approach. The sight of him was so endearing she couldn't bring herself to refuse his offer. "What am I going to do with you?"

"Well, you could start by helping me control Pee-wee. I'm running low on nuggets and he looks like he's about to jump in here with me and make me prove it."

Kara padded barefoot to the truck. "You're crazy, Tyler. These dogs have only met you once. How did you know they wouldn't bite?"

He waved the paper take-out carton. "Bribes. Works every time."

"Oh, sure. As long as you don't run out of food." It amazed Kara how rested, how invigorated, how radiantly alive she suddenly felt. "Did you bring sodas? Napkins?"

"Yup," he answered, holding out his hand to her. "Come on in. The food's getting cold."

Kara climbed into the back of the truck by stepping on the bumper and letting him help her over the tailgate. She had to speak firmly to her dogs to make them stop trying to follow.

Smiling so widely her cheeks hurt, she gazed at the party Tyler had prepared, complete with two folding chairs and a tray-table. "I see you thought of everything."

"I tried to. All that's missing is a fancy tablecloth, candlelight and violins. I was afraid that would be overdoing it."

"Not if you were trying to court me," she said lightly, hoping for a positive response to the blatant cue.

"Which I promised not to do, remember?" he countered. "Here. Sit down. I'll get you a plate and a fork. Nothing but the finest paper and plastic for my guests."

Kara resigned herself to making the most of the precious gift of his presence, however temporary. No matter what eventually came of their friendship, Tyler had made her feel alive again, as if the future was something to look forward to instead of dread. He'd blessed her spirit more than he'd ever know. She'd always be grateful to him for that. Her fondest wish was to know that she'd made a favorable difference in his life, too. Judging by his upbeat mood, she had. All she needed to do now was keep her own feelings at bay and everything would be fine.

By the time Kara and Tyler finished eating, the sun had set and the luminescent green flashes of courting fireflies were starting to appear above the lawn and low shrubs. In the distance, a whippoorwill called.

"Is that one of your Purple Martins I hear?" he asked.

Kara shook her head. "No. They're strictly day-time hunters. Mosquitoes are their favorite food, which is why we can sit out here at night without being bitten."

"Hey, you're right!" Tyler leaned back in his chair, laced his fingers behind his head, and used the edge of the tailgate as a footstool. "Think Martin houses would work if I put them up at my place?"

"Sure. It's probably too late to attract any nesting birds this year but you could always get ready for next spring. Martins migrate to South America to spend the winter. They'll all be gone soon."

"You're kidding."

"No. I mean it." He looked dubious so she added, "I can lend you a book about their habits, if you like. They never nest alone, which is why we put up houses with lots of compartments. Each colony is one big, happy family."

Tyler didn't particularly want to read about big, happy families, even if they were only a bunch of birds. He also didn't like the feelings of affection for Kara that kept popping into his head. Birds had it easy. They just grabbed a mate, made a nest, and that was that. He'd tried to build a family with Deanne and failed. Once was enough.

"I don't need to read a book," Tyler said flatly. "Just tell me what kind of stuff I need and I'll buy it."

"You mean make you a *list?*" Kara saw his color deepen. Even with only moonlight to illuminate the scene, it was evident he was embarrassed.

"Yeah, well...writing all that stuff down was a mistake. I think we should forget about it." The silly list he'd made as a joke had ceased being funny as his personal awareness of Kara had grown. She was a desirable, witty, intelligent, attractive woman. *Too* attractive, considering their pledge to be no more than friends.

Tyler could see he'd made a big mistake by insisting he and Kara spend more time together. The only way to control his impulsive thoughts was to leave, as soon as possible. He got to his feet. "Looks like it's time I went home."

"Awww. The party's over?" The hours had passed swiftly. Kara had no idea how late it was. Nor did she care.

"We both have to get up early tomorrow." Tyler busied himself gathering the residue of their feast and stuffing it into a trash bag. "I'll take this with me so your dogs don't get into it and hurt themselves."

"Okay." Puzzled, Kara handed him an empty carton. For a guy who'd been so insistent that she dine with him, he was sure acting put off all of a sudden. She tried to recall exactly what she'd said or done that had triggered such an adverse reaction. Nothing came to mind. Still, *something* had definitely destroyed their earlier tranquility.

Deciding she should ask what was bothering him, Kara silently rehearsed speech after speech, trying to make up her mind what to say. No approach seemed suitable. Soon, her uncalled-for nervousness had built to such heights she could hardly form a coherent thought.

Her heart fluttered. That unique frame of mind was all too familiar. And decidedly unwelcome. Her body was reacting to Tyler's mood change in *precisely* the same way it had whenever Alex or her father had gotten upset!

That honest analysis absolutely floored her.

Kara was still dealing with the possible ramifications of her disturbing conclusion long after Tyler had driven away.

Chapter Fifteen

Sunday after Sunday, Kara continued to sit with Tyler in church and try to act as if nothing had changed in their so-called relationship. But it had. She'd analyzed her innermost thoughts and decided that, although she did love him, she obviously wasn't trusting him completely. As Susan had pointed out, she wasn't even trusting God the way she should, and she had no idea how to change that, either.

Now that Road Kill's broken leg was healed and the pup no longer needed her care, it was getting easier to avoid Tyler during the week. Sundays, however, were a different story. She'd begun to dread going to church. She knew she could ask Tyler to worship somewhere else, only then he'd wonder why she'd suggested it. Which would mean either lying or admitting her emotions had gotten out-of-control. Neither would do. She was stuck in a no-win situation.

Still, Kara knew she must stop seeing Tyler...anywhere. Period. The more they were together, the harder it was to pretend she didn't care; to behave as if they were just casual friends. Given enough opportunity she was bound to say or do something that revealed how crazy she was about him. Once that happened she'd never be able to face him again. Because he was Mark's boss, that attitude could hurt Susan's family, too.

Thinking about the mess she'd gotten into by agreeing to a supposedly harmless little fib, Kara decided there was no such thing as a harmless lie. She felt like kicking herself. Instead, she simply stuffed her raw emotions into the farthest corners of her mind and refused to show anyone how much she was suffering.

Catching her between patients, Susan was the first to mention the symptoms of her withdrawal. "Hey, Kara." She snapped her fingers. "Wake up. What's the matter with you lately?"

"Nothing. Sorry. What were you saying?" There was no enthusiasm in her tone.

"So," Susan drawled, "you'll give me a big raise?"

Kara's mind jerked back to reality. "What?"

"I figured that would get your attention. I was

actually talking about Ty's hayride idea for the fall festival at church. Do you like it?''

"Sure. The kids will love riding in a wagon."

"So will the adults, if they're anything like Mark and me." She giggled. "Are you working a booth, again?"

"No. I'm not up to it this year." Placing one hand on the small of her back, Kara stretched to ease the strained muscles. "I carted all those boxes of old receipts home so I could rummage through them in the evenings. It's amazing how much trivia we accumulated when Alex was keeping the books. He sure didn't have his act together the way you do."

"Thanks." Susan smiled, then sobered. "I wouldn't be so sure all that confusion was due to his lack of skill, though. I've been going over your personal records, the way you wanted me to, and I suspect the man was a lot smarter than we've given him credit for."

Kara couldn't honestly refute her sister's theory. She had never caught Alex doing anything deliberately unlawful but she had corrected a few mistakes in his accounts once. Soon after, he'd started updating the bills on the computer terminal in his private office.

"Nothing was correctly filed, that's for sure," Kara said. "Trying to put everything in order is a nightmare."

"Are you close to being done?"

"Close enough." She rubbed her back again. "I

think I'll have the job finished this weekend, at the latest.''

"Then what?''

Kara arched her eyebrows and shrugged. "I don't know. Depends on what I find when I start matching our suppliers to the actual usage. I still can't bring myself to believe Alex purposely endangered the Corbett herd—or anyone else's animals—the way Tyler claimed he did.''

"I don't suppose you've asked Tyler for his version of the story, have you?''

"Of course not! Why would I bring that up? You're the one who told me he blames himself for his wife's death.''

"So?''

"So, it all ties together. If his herd hadn't gotten sick he could have sold it off, or used it as instant collateral, instead of borrowing against the ranch property to pay his wife's extra medical expenses. That would have been much faster and easier. Only nobody wanted anything to do with unhealthy cattle.''

"That's not your fault,'' Susan argued.

Nodding, Kara sighed. "I just hope I can prove to myself that it wasn't my husband's fault, either.''

By late Friday night, Kara knew the worst. Alex had bought enough vaccine to cover the Corbett ranch's needs, all right. But he'd also treated a large herd out near Ravenden. That meant he'd either diluted all the vaccine or skipped half the inoculations he'd claimed to have given. Either way, she didn't think she could ever face Tyler again. Truth to tell, she was having enough trouble facing herself. How could she have been so stupid? So naive? So trusting?

She bit her lip as her actual weakness became clear. She'd been cowardly, not stupid. It had been easier to overlook Alex's faults than to face him, incur his wrath and insist on a clear accounting. Which meant she shared the blame for everything.

But what could she do to make amends? *Nothing.* She didn't have the monetary resources to pay anyone back for their losses, no matter how much she wanted to. Nor could she do anything about Tyler's personal hardships. The worst part was knowing he blamed himself for the tragedy Alex's dishonesty had sparked.

In need of comfort, Kara picked up the phone and dialed her sister. The minute Susan answered she blurted out the whole sordid story. When she was through, all her nervous energy had been spent and she plopped into the nearest chair, exhausted.

Susan offered reassurance. ''Don't blame yourself, Kara. You didn't know what was going on.''

''I do now.''

''True, but so what? It's all in the past.''

Slowly, pensively shaking her head, Kara voiced the truth she'd been avoiding. ''No, it's not. I have to tell Tyler. He deserves to know everything, so he can stop blaming himself.''

''Are you sure?''

''Yes.'' She pictured the ruggedly handsome face she'd come to love and imagined the loathing she'd see in his eyes once he heard the truth. ''You and I both know it's the right thing to do,'' Kara said with a shudder. In her heart she knew that facing Tyler and revealing the wrongdoing her search had turned up was absolutely essential.

It would also be the hardest thing she'd ever done.

On the morning of the bazaar, Susan drove her car to church so she could safely transport the cakes she'd baked. Mark rode with Tyler in the rubber-tired ranch wagon. They'd hitched a team of sorrel mules to it and lined it with bales of clean straw to use for benches. Tyler was driving.

''Susie called her sister, just like you wanted,'' Mark said. ''But Kara wouldn't budge. Says she's too busy to come today.'' He plucked a shaft of loose straw, twirled it between his fingers, then stuck one end of it in his mouth. ''I don't know what's gotten into her lately. I haven't seen her act so gloomy in years. Not since—''

''Since her husband was alive?'' Tyler offered.

''Yeah. How'd you know?''

He shrugged. ''I knew her then, too. Not as well as you, of course, but well enough. In those days I never would have guessed she was so smart and funny, and——" He stopped talking when Mark began to laugh.

"You forgot *beautiful*," Mark said. "And *lovable*."

Tyler started to glare at him, then softened. "Yeah. And you forgot *tenderhearted*. I don't know why she insists on taking in all those stray animals."

"I think it's partly because it's her nature to rescue things. Always has been. I suppose that's why she became a veterinarian in the first place."

"What do you know about Alex Shepherd?"

"Not much. I never liked the guy. Don't have a clue why, though. He was always pleasant to me when we ran into each other at family gatherings." Concentrating, Mark squinted and stared off into the distance, then added, "There was just something about him that put up the hackles on the back of my neck the minute he walked into a room. And that was back before I knew he was abusing Kara, so I can't blame my reaction on that."

Tyler stiffened and brought the team to a halt with an abrupt, "Whoa!" When he turned to Mark there was fire in his eyes. "What do you mean he abused Kara? When? How?"

"Hey, don't look at me like that," Mark said, flinching under his angry stare. "I just found out about it a couple of weeks ago, right after she finally told Susie."

"Told her what?"

"That she'd been afraid of Alex. Apparently, he

had the same kind of volatile temper their father used to have. Only Alex was better at hiding it. He saved his tantrums for his wife, when they were alone. One night he went nuts and broke every dish in a fancy set they'd gotten for a wedding present. It was a gift Kara had really loved, so I guess he figured he was punishing her.''

"And Kara put up with behavior like that? I can't believe it.''

"I know what you mean. I had the same problem when Susan first told me. But you have to remember how much Kara has changed since she's been on her own.'' Starting to smile, Mark added, ''She's gotten even more independent since she started seeing you. Obviously, being in love is real good for her morale.''

Tyler's gut knotted. Kara wasn't in love. She'd made it perfectly clear on more than one occasion that she wasn't interested in romance. And no wonder. Thinking about her appalling life with Alex Shepherd made Tyler want to lash out. Since Mark was the only target available, he squelched that urge and replaced it with a more acceptable one. He *had* to see Kara. Immediately. Eyeing the church in the distance, he told Mark, ''Get out.''

"What?''

"You're walking from here. It's not far. A little exercise will do you good. Tell them I'll have the wagon back in plenty of time for the hayride.''

Mark did as he was told. "Okay. You're the boss. Where will you be?"

"I'm going to Kara's."

Grinning knowingly, Mark stepped away to give Tyler room to turn the team. All he said was, "Well, well. What a surprise."

Kara heard the jingle of the mules' harnesses before she actually saw the low-sided wagon turning into her driveway. She quickly called her dogs so they wouldn't spook the team.

Shading her eyes with one hand she recognized her visitor. Apprehension washed over her. "Oh, please, Lord, not yet. I know I asked for the opportunity to tell him the truth, and I will. I promise. But you can't expect me to do it now. I haven't even *begun* to decide what I should say or how I should say it."

Heart beating wildly, Kara watched Tyler's approach. Normally, she would have admired the matched pair of mules. This time, however, she had eyes only for their driver. Tyler's hat was set low, shading his luminous, dark eyes. Strong hands held perfect command of the reins. One boot was propped on the footboard, the other on the brake. The sight of him was so dear, so heart wrenching, it caused her actual physical pain. So did her guilty conscience. She didn't have a clue how she was going to cope with both problems at the same time.

During the drive, Tyler's contemplation about

how Alex had treated Kara had left him so upset he was barely able to curb his temper. He brought the team to a halt a few feet from her. Instead of his usual pleasant greeting, he ordered, "Get in."

His overbearing attitude restored a measure of Kara's lost self-control. By focusing on being miffed she was able to reply with suitable sarcasm. "Good morning to you, too, Mr. Corbett. What brings you here like this?" She gestured at the wagon. "Did your truck break down?"

"I came to get you for the fall doings at church. Mark had some crazy idea you weren't planning to come."

"I'm not." Kara stood her ground.

"And why is that?"

"Because, I…" Hands on her hips, she scowled up at him. "Hey. Hold it, mister. I don't have to explain a thing to you."

Tyler knew she was right. He hadn't meant to come on so strong. Or to start ordering her around, either. He was just so furious and so frustrated by what he'd recently learned from Mark, he hadn't been thinking straight. And now he'd made a bad situation worse.

Wrapping the reins around the wagon brake he climbed down, intent on looking directly into Kara's eyes when he apologized. He had to be sure she didn't fear him the same way she'd feared her late husband. A slightly built woman like Kara would have been crazy to stand up to Alex Shepherd when she'd already seen proof of his violent tendencies. Leave him, yes. Challenge him, no.

All Tyler wanted to do at that moment was take her in his arms, hold her tight and promise to protect her forever. Instead, he stepped closer and solemnly removed his hat. "I'm sorry, Kara. There's no excuse for my lack of manners. Will you do me the honor of letting me drive you to church in my wagon? Please?"

She didn't know what to say or do. In all the times they'd been together she'd never seen him act so earnest. When he added a second, "Please?" it was hard to refuse.

"I have a lot of chores to do," she alibied. "I really can't spare the time."

Placing his hand gently on her shoulder he felt her flinch. The unconscious reaction to being touched tore him up inside. Speaking softly, comfortingly, he reassured her. "You don't have to be afraid of me, Kara. I'd never, ever hurt you. I swear it. As God is my witness." There was a quick flash of doubt in her upturned gaze. It was replaced by a subtle yet perceptive smile that reached into Tyler's soul and calmed his uneasiness.

"I know." Kara slipped her arms around his waist and stepped into his waiting embrace. Laying her cheek on his chest she listened to the heavy, reassuring beat of his heart. If she could have stayed there like that for the rest of her days, she'd have gladly done so. Unfortunately, that was impossible.

Acting lighthearted to keep Tyler from seeing how deeply his vow had touched her, she leaned back and smiled up at him. "I suppose this means you'll expect me to give in and go with you now?"

"Only if you want to." He brushed a conciliatory kiss on her forehead. "I've been praying hard that you'd change your mind, though."

She rolled her eyes dramatically. "Oh, great! So, if I refuse you, you'll blame me for undermining your faith?"

"It could happen."

Kara watched his grin spread, crinkling the corners of his eyes. This was the kind of cheerful give-and-take she'd missed so much when she'd stopped spending extra time with him. She knew it was foolish to resume the sham relationship that had already caused her to lose her heart, yet the urge to allow herself a few more hours with him was very strong. Besides, she reasoned, if they spent the day at the church get-together, maybe she'd have a chance to explain what Alex had done.

Kara sighed. Who was she kidding? All she wanted was the opportunity to enjoy a few more special moments with the man she loved. To make memories that no one could ever take away. Once Tyler learned who had been responsible for his loss, there was no way he'd ever be able to look at her again and not remember, not think the worst.

"All right. I'll go," Kara said, feigning a casual attitude. "Give me a few minutes to change."

"Why? You look fine to me."

The compliment made her feel like she'd just been handed first place in a beauty contest. "Thanks. You're not so bad yourself, cowboy."

"It's the hat," Tyler quipped, squaring it on his head. "Gets 'em every time." He held out his hand. "Come on. Let's go before you change your mind."

"I won't change my mind," Kara promised. "But I do intend to change to newer jeans. If I go to the church in these, my friends are liable to take up a collection to clothe me!"

"If you ask me, you'd even look good in a feed sack," he insisted, "but I won't argue. Just hurry. A lot of kids are waiting for hayrides. I don't want to disappoint them."

"Right. Be back in a flash."

Kara was still reeling from his compliments as she ran toward the house. Could he have meant them, or was he just being polite to add emphasis to his apology for being so grumpy? It had to be the latter. After all, he'd been married to Deanne, a tall, beautiful blond who looked like an angel and was so perfect she was practically a saint.

"And I'm neither," Kara grumbled to herself. "I could lighten my hair but I'd still be short. And seriously imperfect."

She grimaced. It was a good thing God loved her, no matter what, because even after surrendering to His will and becoming a Christian, she still had plenty of flaws left.

* * *

Halfway to the church, Kara was so convicted she had to speak out or explode. "Tyler?"

"Mm-hm."

"There's something I have to tell you." When he glanced over at her and opened his mouth to speak, she shushed him. "No. Be quiet and just listen. I don't know if I can get through this if you talk to me."

"You don't have to explain anything. I already know all about Alex," he said softly.

Kara was awestruck. "You do?"

"Yes. Mark told me this morning. He said Susan confided in him. I suppose most married couples would do the same." After a soul-wrenching sigh he went on. "Dee and I never managed to reach that point. She had the idiotic notion she was supposed to hide the bad stuff from me, for my own good. That's why I didn't find out how sick she really was until it was already too late."

"Oh, Tyler, I'm so sorry. For everything." Kara reached out to him and laid her hand over his as he gripped the reins. He didn't look at her but she could see his eyes glistening with tears.

"I guess that's why I was so upset this morning. Why didn't you tell me what your marriage was like?"

"What good would that have done? I didn't want to be pitied. Besides, I had to admit my weaknesses, and Alex's, before I could hope to overcome anything." Her fingers gently stroked the back of Tyler's hand as she rested her head on his shoulder. "I thought I'd never..."

Kara wanted to say she'd thought she'd never fall in love again, but now that she fully comprehended the significance of Tyler's promise that he'd never hurt her, she realized there was far more to her change of heart than mere romantic love.

"Go on," he urged.

Kara was so relieved, so joyful, she didn't know where to begin. "Oh, Tyler. I can't believe how blessed I am. I didn't think I'd ever meet a man I could trust the way I trust you. After what Alex did, I was sure you wouldn't want to have anything more to do with me. But here we are. Still together. It's a miracle. I can't wait to get to church and tell Susan!"

He chuckled. "Then I suppose you don't want me to stop this wagon and give you a kiss, huh?"

"Nope," Kara said, laughing with him. "I want at least *two* kisses. And that's just for starters."

As soon as Tyler released the reins she fell into his arms, gave up the last of her reservations against loving him, and lifted her face to his.

Tyler's kiss was gentle at first, then grew more and more demanding. Kara's head spun. Her heart raced. Her soul rejoiced. This was not the kind of intimate awareness she'd expected when she'd released the last of her misgivings and admitted how much she loved him. This was truer, deeper, absolutely flawless. It was unexplainable. Unfathomable.

Kara closed her eyes and returned his kiss with every ounce of her being. Surely, no woman in the entire universe had ever been as happy as she was at that moment.

Chapter Sixteen

The churchyard was decorated with bundles of
dried cornstalks, gourds, squash and pumpkins.
Streamers of crepe paper in rich autumn colors hung
from the trees and fluttered in the breeze amid the
falling leaves.

As soon as Tyler brought the wagon to a halt, he
was mobbed by giggling, tussling, shouting children.

Kara reluctantly left him and went looking for her
sister. She found her in the church kitchen with three
other women, slicing cakes and pies into individual
servings.

Everyone was startled when Kara burst through
the door and screeched, "Susan! Guess what just
happened."

"From the look on your face, it must be something pretty good." She laid down her knife, licked

icing from her fingers, then rinsed her hands in the sink.

"Not good...wonderful!" Kara rushed to join her. "I just left Tyler. You won't believe this. He's not mad. Not at all."

"About what?"

"About Alex, of course." She lowered her voice. "I didn't expect you to tell Mark right away but now I'm glad you did. He blabbed the whole thing to Tyler this morning. I didn't have to explain a thing. Isn't that terrific?"

"Whoa." Susan took her by the arm and led her to a distant corner of the room where they could talk more privately. "Slow down and start from the beginning. What makes you think Tyler knows what Alex did?"

"He said so."

"In so many words?"

Kara's brow knit. "Well, no. I guess not. But I'm sure he knows. He said you'd told Mark all about it." She didn't like the additional sympathy that had begun to color her sister's already concerned expression.

"Mark was in bed, snoring, when you and I talked on the phone last night," Susan said. "The guy sleeps like a rock. I couldn't have tattled on Alex if I'd wanted to."

"Surely this morning..."

She shook her head. "No. Mark grabbed his breakfast on the run and headed for the barn so he could get his chores done early and ride into town with Tyler.''

"That's not right. It can't be. Tyler was alone in the wagon when he came to pick me up.''

"I know. They were almost to the church when he made Mark get out and walk the rest of the way. That's really all I know, except that my poor husband was grumbling about his sore feet by the time he finally got here.''

Dizzy, Kara leaned against the wall for support. If only she could recall exactly what she'd said to Tyler. Or what he'd said to her. Her thoughts were a hopeless jumble being stirred by a growing sense of foreboding. What a fool she'd made of herself, babbling on and on about how wonderful Tyler was! When he *did* find out the truth, he'd probably imagine she'd only kissed him to keep him from demanding restitution for his losses. Not that she'd blame him. If she were in his shoes, that's *exactly* what she'd think.

Susan slid a comforting arm around her shoulders. "I'm sorry, Kara. Don't you see? It couldn't have been Alex's dishonesty that you and Tyler were talking about this morning. Mark doesn't know about it, yet.''

See? Oh, yes, she saw plenty. In the shattered mirror of her mind everything was becoming agonizingly clear. "I guess it must have been Alex's awful temper that Tyler meant. It all makes perfect sense now that I think about it. That's what made him say he'd never hurt me." Her lower lip quivered with repressed emotion. "Too bad he isn't going to be able to keep that promise."

"Maybe…" Susan began.

Kara interrupted her. "No. It's over. You know it and I know it, so don't try to kid me."

"What are you going to do?"

"What should I do? Go home? Forget him? Forget about dreaming of having his children?" Tears crested her lower lashes and trickled down her cheeks. Sniffling and fighting the urge to sob out loud, she added, "If I live to be a hundred, I know I'll never be able to forget him. Never stop loving him."

When Susan opened her arms to offer a motherly hug, Kara lost her battle with her raw emotions and collapsed on her sister's shoulder, weeping as if she'd just lost her best friend. As far as she was concerned, that was exactly what had happened.

Time with the children was so hectic it was after twelve before Tyler realized how long it had been since Kara had left him. He passed the reins to Mark and went looking for her. Instead, he ran into Susan.

"Hi. Have you seen Kara? She was supposed to come back and ride the hay wagon with me after she talked to you." Grinning, he pushed his hat off his forehead and wiped his brow. "I need her help. Those kids are tough to handle."

"I haven't seen her for hours," Susan said flatly.

"But don't worry about Kara. She can take care of herself."

"Not according to Mark."

Her eyebrows arched. "So he did tell you something. That explains a lot." She pointed to some chairs in the shade next to the old stone building. "I think you'd better sit down. Apparently, you only know half the story."

"Okay. Sure." Concerned, Tyler offered Susan a chair, then spun another one around backward and straddled it like a horse, facing her. "What else is there? Mark already told me Alex used to lose his temper and scare the fire out of Kara." He stiffened, scowling. "He didn't hit her, did he?"

"No, but he might as well have. If that man were alive right now and I caught him in a dark alley, he'd be real sorry." She folded her arms across her chest, made a dour face and snorted in disgust. "I guess I might as well get this over with. Remember this morning, when you and Kara were talking? She thought you meant you weren't angry that Alex had shorted you when he vaccinated your herd."

Tyler was on his feet in a heartbeat, sending the chair flying. "What? Is that true?"

"I'm afraid so. Somehow, Kara got the idea Mark had already told you all about it. Only he couldn't have. She didn't phone me with the bad news until late last night, long after Mark had gone to bed. There was no way to change history, so I didn't wake him."

Tyler couldn't believe what he was hearing. Indignation hardened his heart. "And what about *before?* How long has Kara known about this? Months? Years? Since it happened?"

Susan stood rigid and returned his anger in kind. "If you really think that, then I'm glad you and Kara are through. She was married to one stinker. She doesn't need another husband like that, now or ever."

"Who said anything about us getting married?" he shouted. "Kara and I were just pretending to like each other in the first place!"

Their raised voices had attracted a crowd but Susan didn't back down. "Look. Kara already knows she was a fool to fall for you. She always was too naive, too loving, too empathetic. That's her biggest problem. She never did have enough sense to turn away lonely, helpless critters when she thought they needed her."

"Meaning *me,* I suppose? Well, I'm not lonely. And I'm not helpless, either," Tyler snapped.

"Oh, yeah? If you're so sure of yourself, then why are you yelling?"

Like it or not, he had no ready answer.

Susan nodded and stared at him knowingly. "That's what I thought. How long have you been in love with my sister?"

"I'm not…"

"Careful, Tyler," she drawled, "you're standing in a churchyard. I don't think it's a very good idea

to tell a fib here...or anywhere else, for that matter.''
The moment she detected a softening in his expression, she stepped closer and laid a hand on his arm.
''Kara didn't know what Alex had done until she'd
finished sorting out some old statements he'd left
behind. It was only late yesterday that she had
enough information to put it all together.''

Tyler realized he'd been holding his breath as Susan spoke. He exhaled with a whoosh. ''Why didn't
she *tell* me?''

''She thought that's what you two were discussing on the ride down here. I was the one who had
to break her heart and explain she was mistaken.''

He glanced into the crowd of onlookers, searching
in vain. ''I have to talk to her. Where is she?''

''I don't know. I suppose she went home to lick
her wounds. Personally, I'd have run as far away as
I could get, but Kara's not like that. I hope you
realize how easy it would have been for her to destroy the old bills and hide the real truth from all of
us.''

''I'm beginning to see a lot of things I missed
before,'' Tyler said soberly. ''Can I borrow your
car?''

''Why?''

''Because I'm temporarily afoot. Unless you expect me to chase after Kara in the hay wagon. If
she's not at home, it could take me forever to catch
up to her that way.''

Susan began to smile. ''Oh, I don't know. The

cowboy heroes in the movies always manage to arrive in time to rescue the damsels in distress.'' The consternation in his expression made her giggle. ''Of course, they usually ride beautiful white horses. The scene might lose some of its romance if you trotted up to her driving two other jackasses... besides yourself, that is.''

''That's another reason I'd rather take your car,'' Tyler countered wryly, ''so Kara doesn't get me mixed up with the mules. We're all stubborn and hardheaded. Considering the ridiculous mistakes I've made recently, I don't want to take the chance she might get the three of us confused.''

Kara was so engrossed in cleaning the barn she didn't hear Susan's car approach. Her first clue that she was no longer alone was a tall shadow falling across her path.

Startled, she spun around and gasped. That was enough to bring Peewee to her side, growling a warning until he recognized their visitor.

Tyler paused and calmly held out his hands. ''It's just me, Kara. I didn't mean to scare you. I knocked on your front door. Nobody answered.'' He chanced a slight smile. ''I figured I'd find you wherever all the animals were gathered. And sure enough, here you are.''

Realizing she'd pushed herself to exhaustion as a temporary means of taking her mind off her troubles, she leaned wearily on the handle of the pitchfork. "I know why *I'm* here. The question is, why are *you* here?"

"To finish what we started this morning."

Kara drew one wrist across her forehead to push back wisps of damp hair, then shook her head sadly. "Look, Tyler, I've been giving this whole mess a lot of thought. I made a big mistake this morning. I guess I wanted to believe I could get away with not telling you something important because I didn't want to be the one to hurt you. So I interpreted our conversation to my advantage. Only it wasn't. To my advantage, I mean."

His smile widened. "Are you through?"

"No. I have to explain. It's just very hard to do."

"I can see that."

"I'll bet you can," she countered. "Will you please take me seriously and stop that silly grinning?"

"Honey, I'll take you any way I can get you," Tyler said with clear affection. Approaching, he held out his hand. "But first, I want you to put down the pitchfork." He eased it from her hand and laid it aside before continuing. "Susan told me everything. And I mean, *everything*."

When Kara tried to speak he silenced her by placing one finger lightly across her lips. "Hush. I admit I was pretty mad, at first. Who wouldn't be? But I thought it all through on my way over here. It wasn't your fault. I don't want us to ever talk about what

Alex did or didn't do again, in private or in his veterinary practice. None of that matters."

"Yes, it does." Kara's voice quavered, her eyes filling with unshed tears.

"Only if we let it," he insisted. "Neither one of us had a perfect marriage, in spite of what we led people to believe." Seeing the doubt in her eyes he added, "No. Not even me. If my wife had trusted me, loved me the way you do, she'd have known it was unfair to withhold a portion of her life, simply because the details weren't pretty. Keeping me in the dark like that wasn't a kindness. It was cruel and unfair."

Kara placed her palms on Tyler's broad chest. His arms encircled her. Pleading for understanding with her gaze, she said, "Alex and I ran the animal hospital together. I should have kept closer track of the details. Maybe I could have stopped him."

"You know that kind of a man wouldn't have paid any attention to your moral objections, even if you had figured out the hoax he was pulling. I thank God you didn't realize what was going on. Alex could have hurt you—or worse—if he saw you as a threat to his schemes."

Tyler's arms tightened, pulling Kara closer, protecting her from unseen danger simply because he loved her so deeply, so completely, he could do no less.

She wrapped her arms around his waist and laid her cheek on his chest. Their heartbeats merged, became one rhythm, as if the Lord were joining them to each other, body and soul. Maybe Tyler was right. Maybe God had kept her blinded to the truth for her own sake. This was the first time she'd considered the possibility of being in her heavenly Father's safekeeping all along.

And now? Kara wondered. She started to rehearse what she should say to Tyler, then realized it was unnecessary. No longer worried, she tilted her head back and looked up at him without reservation. The sight of his dear face thrilled her beyond belief. It was a good thing he was holding her so close because she doubted her wobbly legs would support her if he let go.

Happiness and perfect peace flowed over, around and through her. She grinned at him through a mist of joy. "Hey, cowboy?"

"Yes, ma'am?"

"Are you just going to stand there, or are you going to kiss me?"

"I could do that," Tyler drawled. "But first I want to ask you something."

"Talk, talk, talk. That's all we seem to do." To Kara's delight he silenced her with a long, firm kiss that stole her breath away. She was still struggling to regain her equilibrium when he began to whisper against her cheek.

"I was going to ask you to marry me, but if you don't want to talk..."

Wide-eyed, Kara leaned back and stared at him. "I—I might be willing to make an exception."

"That's mighty gracious of you," Tyler teased. "Well?"

"You're really serious about this? I mean, you're not going to let me answer, then laugh hysterically and tell me it was all a joke, are you?"

She saw his countenance start to darken and began waving her hands in front of her as if she could shoo her words away like pesky gnats. "Never mind. Forget I said that. I'm a little nervous, that's all. I never thought I'd even *consider* getting married again, and now, here I am with—"

Tyler interrupted. "Was that a *yes*? I couldn't tell."

"Yes!" she squealed, throwing her arms around his neck. "Yes, yes, yes."

Tyler caught her up and spun them both in circles. Sharing the excitement, Kara's dogs began barking and running back and forth. The little terrier dashed up and nipped at Tyler's ankle, giving the leg of his pants a good thrashing. Thanks to his boots, he wasn't hurt.

He set Kara on her feet and pointed down. "Um, would you mind explaining to your furry friends that I'm one of the good guys? They seem to be confused."

"Whiskers!" Kara scooped the terrier up and spoke to him like a naughty child. "Shame on you. That's your new daddy. You can't bite him anymore.'' Elated and giddy, she knew she was grinning comically but she didn't care. She set the dog down and turned to Tyler. ''There. How was that?''

''Wonderful.'' He gently cupped her cheek, then slid his fingers into her silky hair and drew her closer. ''Is there any way I can break you of making me surrogate daddy to all of your pets?''

Kara immediately thought of the very personal dream she'd confessed to Susan back at the church. In the past, she'd have kept the idea of having children to herself and hoped Tyler would eventually guess what she was thinking, what she wanted.

Now, however, she blurted out her reply before she had a chance to modify it. Or to change her mind. ''Well, I suppose...if you were a *real* daddy, it wouldn't seem quite so appropriate.'' The passion lighting Tyler's eyes told her she'd done the right thing by speaking her mind.

''I'd love that. I've always wanted kids,'' he said softly, tenderly. ''I guess there are a lot of other important things you and I need to settle, too, before we get married. I don't want to rush you into anything.''

Kara's smile was so expansive her cheek muscles were beginning to ache. ''Oh, really? Shucks. Then I suppose next week would be too soon for the wedding, huh?'' The look of astonishment on his face made her giggle. ''Okay, okay. I'll give you a little more time if you insist. How about two weeks? I don't know if I can stand waiting three. I've been really, *really* lonesome. Especially lately."

"Oh? Why is that?"

She playfully punched him in the shoulder. "Stop grinning at me like that. You know perfectly well what I mean. I'm tired of cooking dinner for one. And coming home to a dark house. And not having anybody but the animals to talk to at night. And..." Blushing, she broke off.

Tyler finished the sentence for her. "And sleeping alone? Me, too. Come on." Tyler slid his arm around her shoulders and guided her out of the barn.

Kara was afraid he'd gotten the wrong idea until he stopped at Susan's car and opened the passenger door. She got in. "Where are we going?"

"To round up a best man and matron of honor, reserve the church and tell the preacher what we have in mind," he said, joining her. "How long is it going to take you to find a wedding dress?"

"I'd get married in denim if I had to, as long as you were the groom." She scooted over close to him and laid her hand on his thigh as if it were the most natural gesture in the world. Somehow, it felt like they'd always been together. Always been a couple.

Tyler put his hand over hers. "Did I mention how much I love you?"

"How should I know? I hardly remember my own name when I'm around you."

His laugh was rich and deep. "I know what you mean. After your sister told me why you'd left the festival, I decided to chase after you before I realized I didn't have a car! That's why I borrowed this one."

"I suppose we could drive back separately so you could return Susan's car and I'd have a way home," Kara suggested logically.

"No way, lady. We don't need any other transportation when we have a perfectly good wagon and team waiting for us back at the church. You and I are taking a nice, slow hayride in the moonlight tonight. I might even stop once in a while and give you a few more kisses, if that's okay with you."

"It's *very* okay." Kara snuggled closer to him and sighed. This was turning out to be a wonderful day, and he'd promised her an equally wonderful evening.

With a start like that, and a man like Tyler to love her, the rest of her life was bound to be blessed.

No one could ask for more.

*   *   *   *   *

Dear Reader,

There are many decisions in life that can help make the difference between success or failure, health or illness, joy or sadness. But in the final analysis, no matter how hard we struggle or how much we scheme, we're still not in charge of the final outcome. We never were.

Do we always understand why things happen the way they do? Of course not. Maybe that's why it's so easy to get caught up in worrying about our personal problems and forget that we don't have to face *any* of them alone. Not only does Jesus promise to send the Holy Spirit to comfort us, God also uses perceptive, empathetic people to help us bear our daily burdens. There is no adversity that others have not already successfully overcome, thanks to their faith in Christ.

Sad or happy, our past is a part of us. It never goes away. There's not a thing we can do to change it. But our future is another story. There, we have a choice. We can spend the rest of our days struggling through life alone, or we can reach out to the Lord, turn our lives over to Him, and be assured He will never forsake us.

Jesus is waiting to wrap us in His loving arms and heal our broken hearts. All we have to do is let Him.

Valerie Hansen

Valerie Hansen
P.O. Box 13
Glencoe, AR 72539-0013